HAMILTON
on the hunt

His best friend had overdosed on ecstasy . . . and the cops called it suicide. Hamilton had other ideas—but proving them might cost him his life!

The defenseless, frozen dead were being robbed of their organs. Everybody seemed to know it . . . but nobody cared. Then the rip-offs began on the living . . . and Hamilton became a target!

Tracking down illegitimate breeders to enforce the Fertility Laws seemed pretty routine. Then the chase ran off course and led Hamilton into the most insidious death design of all!

3 Fabulous SF/Detective Novellas

Also by Larry Niven
Published by Ballantine Books:

ALL THE MYRIAD WAYS
CONVERGENT SERIES
FLIGHT OF THE HORSE
THE FLYING SORCERERS (with David Gerrold)
A GIFT FROM EARTH
A HOLE IN SPACE
NEUTRON STAR
THE PROTECTOR
RINGWORLD
THE RINGWORLD ENGINEERS
TALES OF KNOWN SPACE:
    The Universe of Larry Niven
WORLD OF PTAVVS
A WORLD OUT OF TIME

The Long ARM of Gil Hamilton

Larry Niven

A Del Rey Book

BALLANTINE BOOKS • NEW YORK

A Del Rey Book
Published by Ballantine Books

Copyright © 1976 by Larry Niven

ACKNOWLEDGMENTS
"Death by Ecstasy," Copyright © 1969 (as "The Organleggers") by Galaxy Publishing Corp., for *Galaxy Magazine*, January 1969.

"The Defenseless Dead," Copyright © 1973 by Fawcett Publications for *Ten Tomorrows*.

"ARM," Copyright © 1975 by Robert Silverberg and Roger Elwood for *Epoch*.

Library of Congress Catalog Card Number: 75-35969

ISBN 0-345-30050-5

Printed in Canada

First Edition: February 1976
Seventh Printing: July 1984

First Canadian Printing: March 1976

Cover art by George Bush

CONTENTS

The Long ARM
of Gil Hamilton

DEATH by ECSTASY

First came the routine request for a Breach of Privacy permit. A police officer took down the details and forwarded the request to a clerk, who saw that the tape reached the appropriate civic judge. The judge was reluctant, for privacy is a precious thing in a world of eighteen billion; but in the end he could find no reason to refuse. On November 2, 2123, he granted the permit.

The tenant's rent was two weeks in arrears. If the manager of Monica Apartments had asked for eviction he would have been refused. But Owen Jennison did not answer his doorbell or his room phone. Nobody could recall seeing him in many weeks. Apparently the manager only wanted to know that he was all right.

And so he was allowed to use his passkey, with an officer standing by.

And so they found the tenant of 1809.

And when they had looked in his wallet, they called me.

I was at my desk at ARM Headquarters, making useless notes and wishing it were lunchtime.

At this stage the Loren case was all correlate-and-wait. It involved an organlegging gang, apparently run by a single man, yet big enough to cover half the North American west coast. We had considerable data on the gang—methods of operation, centers of activity, a few former customers, even a tentative handful of names—but nothing that would give us an excuse to act. So it was a matter of shoving what we had into the computer, watching the few suspected associates of the ganglord Loren, and waiting for a break.

1

The months of waiting were ruining my sense of involvement.

My phone buzzed.

I put the pen down and said, "Gil Hamilton."

A small dark face regarded me with soft black eyes. "I am Detective-Inspector Julio Ordaz of the Los Angeles Police Department. Are you related to an Owen Jennison?"

"Owen? No, we're not related. Is he in trouble?"

"You do know him, then."

"Sure I know him. Is he here, on Earth?"

"It would seem so." Ordaz had no accent, but the lack of colloquialisms in his speech made him sound vaguely foreign. "We will need positive identification, Mr. Hamilton. Mr. Jennison's ident lists you as next of kin."

"That's funny. I—back up a minute. Is Owen dead?"

"Somebody is dead, Mr. Hamilton. He carried Mr. Jennison's ident in his wallet."

"Okay. Now, Owen Jennison was a citizen of the Belt. This may have interworld complications. That makes it ARM's business. Where's the body?"

"We found him in an apartment rented under his own name. Monica Apartments, Lower Los Angeles, room 1809."

"Good. Don't move anything you haven't moved already. I'll be right over."

Monica Apartments was a nearly featureless concrete block, eighty stories tall, a thousand feet across the edges of its square base. Lines of small balconies gave the sides a sculptured look, above a forty-foot inset ledge that would keep tenants from dropping objects on pedestrians. A hundred buildings just like it made Lower Los Angeles look lumpy from the air.

Inside, a lobby done in anonymous modern. Lots of metal and plastic showing; lightweight, comfortable chairs without arms; big ashtrays; plenty of indirect lighting; a low ceiling; no wasted space. The whole room might have been stamped out with a die. It wasn't supposed to look small, but it did, and that warned you what the rooms would be like. You'd pay your rent by the cubic centimeter.

I found the manager's office, and the manager, a soft-looking man with watery blue eyes. His conservative paper suit, dark red, seemed chosen to render him invisible, as did the style of his brown hair, worn long and combed straight back without a part. "Nothing like this has ever happened here," he confided as he led me to the elevator banks. "Nothing. It would have been bad enough without his being a Belter, but *now*—" He cringed at the thought. "Newsmen. They'll *smother* us."

The elevator was coffin-sized, but with the handrails on the inside. It went up fast and smooth. I stepped out into a long, narrow hallway.

What would Owen have been doing in a place like this? Machinery lived here, not people.

Maybe it wasn't Owen. Ordaz had been reluctant to commit himself. Besides, there's no law against picking pockets. You couldn't enforce such a law on this crowded planet. Everyone on Earth was a pickpocket.

Sure. Someone had died carrying Owen's wallet.

I walked down the hallway to 1809.

It was Owen who sat grinning in the armchair. I took one good look at him, enough to be sure, and then I looked away and didn't look back. But the rest of it was even more unbelievable.

No Belter could have taken that apartment. I was born in Kansas; but even I felt the awful anonymous chill. It would have driven Owen bats.

"I don't believe it," I said.

"Did you know him well, Mr. Hamilton?"

"About as well as two men can know each other. He and I spent three years mining rocks in the main asteroid belt. You don't keep secrets under those conditions."

"Yet you didn't know he was on Earth."

"That's what I can't understand. Why the blazes didn't he phone me if he was in trouble?"

"You're an ARM," said Ordaz. "An operative in the United Nations Police."

He had a point. Owen was as honorable as any man I knew; but honor isn't the same in the Belt. Belters think flatlanders are all crooks. They don't understand that to a flatlander, picking pockets is a game of skill. Yet a Belter sees smuggling as the same kind of game, with no dishonesty involved. He balances the thirty percent tariff against possible confiscation of his cargo, and if the odds are right he gambles.

Owen could have been doing something that would look honest to him but not to me.

"He could have been in something sticky," I admitted. "But I can't see him killing himself over it. And . . . not here. He wouldn't have come here."

1809 was a living room and a bathroom and a closet. I'd glanced into the bathroom, knowing what I would find. It was the size of a comfortable shower stall. An adjustment panel outside the door would cause it to extrude various appurtenances in memory plastic, to become a washroom, a shower stall, a toilet, a dressing room, a steam cabinet. Luxurious in everything but size, as long as you pushed the right buttons.

The living room was more of the same. A King bed was invisible behind a wall. The kitchen alcove, with basin and oven and grill and toaster, would fold into another wall; the sofa, chairs, and tables would vanish into the floor. One tenant and three guests would make a crowded cocktail party, a cozy dinner gathering, a closed poker game. Card table, dinner table, coffee table were all there, surrounded by the appropriate chairs; but only one set at a time would emerge from the floor. There was no refrigerator, no freezer, no bar. If a tenant needed food or drink he phoned down, and the supermarket on the third floor would send it up.

The tenant of such an apartment had his comfort. But he owned nothing. There was room for him; there was none for his possessions. This was one of the inner apartments. An age ago there would have been an air shaft; but air shafts took up expensive room. The tenant didn't even have a window. He lived in a comfortable box.

Just now the items extruded were the overstuffed reading armchair, two small side tables, a footstool, and the kitchen alcove. Owen Jennison sat grinning in the armchair. Naturally he grinned. Little more than dried skin covered the natural grin of his skull.

"It's a small room," said Ordaz, "but not too small. Millions of people live this way. In any case a Belter would hardly be a claustrophobe."

"No. Owen flew a singleship before he joined us. Three months at a stretch, in a cabin so small you couldn't stand up with the airlock closed. Not claustrophobia, but—" I swept my arm about the room. "What do you see that's his?"

Small as it was, the closet was nearly empty. A set of street clothes, a paper shirt, a pair of shoes, a small brown overnight case. All new. The few items in the bathroom medicine chest had been equally new and equally anonymous.

Ordaz said, "Well?"

"Belters are transients. They don't own much, but what they do own, they guard. Small possessions, relics, souvenirs. I can't believe he wouldn't have had *something*."

Ordaz lifted an eyebrow. "His space suit?"

"You think that's unlikely? It's not. The inside of his pressure suit is a Belter's home. Sometimes it's the only home he's got. He spends a fortune decorating it. If he loses his suit, he's not a Belter anymore.

"No, I don't insist he'd have brought his suit. But he'd have had *something*. His phial of Marsdust. The bit of nickel-iron they took out of his chest. Or, if he left all his souvenirs home, he'd have picked up things on Earth. But in this room—there's *nothing*."

"Perhaps," Ordaz suggested delicately, "he didn't notice his surroundings."

And somehow that brought it all home.

Owen Jennison sat grinning in a water-stained silk dressing gown. His space-darkened face lightened abruptly beneath his chin, giving way to normal suntan. His blond hair, too long, had been cut Earth style; no trace remained of the Belter strip cut he'd worn all his life. A month's growth of untended beard covered half his face. A small black cylinder protruded from the top of his head. An electric cord trailed from the top of the cylinder and ran to a wall socket.

The cylinder was a droud, a current addict's transformer.

I stepped closer to the corpse and bent to look. The droud was a standard make, but it had been altered. Your standard current addict's droud will pass only a trickle of current into the brain. Owen must have been getting ten times the usual charge, easily enough to damage his brain in a month's time.

I reached out and touched the droud with my imaginary hand.

Ordaz was standing quietly beside me, letting me make my examination without interruption. Naturally he had no way of knowing about my restricted psi powers.

With my imaginary fingertips I touched the droud in Owen's head, then ran them down to a tiny hole in his scalp, and further.

It was a standard surgical job. Owen could have had it done anywhere. A hole in his scalp, invisible under the hair, nearly impossible to find even if you knew what you were looking for. Even your best friends wouldn't know, unless they caught you with the droud plugged in. But the tiny hole marked a bigger plug set in the bone of the skull. I touched the ecstasy plug with my imaginary fingertips, then ran them down the hair-fine wire going deep into Owen's brain, down into the pleasure center.

No, the extra current hadn't killed him. What had killed Owen was his lack of will power. He had been unwilling to get up.

He had starved to death sitting in that chair. There were plastic squeezebottles all around his feet, and a couple still on the end tables. All empty. They must have been full a month ago. Owen hadn't died of thirst. He had died of starvation, and his death had been planned.

Owen my crewmate. Why hadn't he come to me? I'm half a Belter myself. Whatever his trouble, I'd have gotten him out somehow. A little smuggling—what of it? Why had he arranged to tell me only after it was over?

The apartment was so clean, so clean. You had to bend close to smell the death; the air conditioning whisked it all away.

He'd been very methodical. The kitchen was open so that a catheter could lead from Owen to the sink. He'd given himself enough water to last out the month; he'd paid his rent a month in advance. He'd cut the droud cord by hand, and he'd cut it short, deliberately tethering himself to a wall socket beyond reach of the kitchen.

A complex way to die, but rewarding in its way. A month of ecstasy, a month of the highest physical pleasure man can attain. I could imagine him giggling every time he remembered he was starving to death. With food only a few footsteps away . . . but he'd have to pull out the droud to reach it. Perhaps he postponed the decision, and postponed it again . . .

Owen and I and Homer Chandrasekhar, we had lived for three years in a cramped shell surrounded by vacuum. What was there to know about Owen Jennison that I hadn't known? Where was the weakness we didn't share? If Owen had done this, so could I. And I was afraid.

"Very neat," I whispered. "Belter neat."

"Typically Belter, would you say?"

"I would not. Belters don't commit suicide. Certainly not this way. If a Belter had to go, he'd blow his ship's drive and die like a star. The neatness is typical. The result isn't."

"Well," said Ordaz. "Well." He was uncomfortable. The facts spoke for themselves, yet he was reluctant to call me a liar. He fell back on formality.

"Mr. Hamilton, do you identify this man as Owen Jennison?"

"It's him." He'd always been a touch overweight, yet I'd recognized him the moment I saw him. "But let's be sure." I pulled the dirty dressing gown back from Owen's shoulder. A near-perfect circle of scar tissue, eight inches across, spread over the left side of his chest. "See that?"

"We noticed it, yes. An old burn?"

"Owen's the only man I know who could show you a meteor scar on his skin. It blasted him in the shoulder one day while he was outside the ship. Sprayed vaporized pressure-suit steel all over his skin. The doc pulled a tiny grain of nickel-iron from the center of the scar, just below the skin. Owen always carried that grain of nickel-iron. Always," I said, looking at Ordaz.

"We didn't find it."

"Okay."

"I'm sorry to put you through this, Mr. Hamilton. It was you who insisted we leave the body *in situ*."

"Yes. Thank you."

Owen grinned at me from the reading chair. I felt the pain, in my throat and in the pit of my stomach. Once I had lost my right arm. Losing Owen felt the same way.

"I'd like to know more about this," I said. "Will you let me know the details as soon as you get them?"

"Of course. Through the ARM office?"

"Yes." This wasn't ARM business, despite what I'd told Ordaz; but ARM prestige would help. "I want to know why Owen died. Maybe he just cracked up . . . culture shock or something. But if someone hounded him to death, I'll have his blood."

"Surely the administration of justice is better left to —" Ordaz stopped, confused. Did I speak as an ARM or as a citizen?

I left him wondering.

The lobby held a scattering of tenants, entering and leaving elevators or just sitting around. I stood outside the elevator for a moment, searching passing faces for the erosion of personality that must be there.

Mass-produced comfort. Room to sleep and eat and watch tridee, but no room to *be* anyone. Living here, one would own nothing. What kind of people would live like that? They should have looked all alike, moved in unison, like the string of images in a barber's mirrors.

Then I spotted wavy brown hair and a dark red paper suit. The manager? I had to get close before I was sure. His face was the face of a permanent stranger.

He saw me coming and smiled without enthusiasm. "Oh, hello, Mr. . . . uh . . . Did you find . . ." He couldn't think of the right question.

"Yes," I said, answering it anyway. "But I'd like to know some things. Owen Jennison lived here for six weeks, right?"

"Six weeks and two days, before we opened his room."

"Did he ever have visitors?"

The man's eyebrows went up. We'd drifted in the direction of his office, and I was close enough to read the name on the door: JASPER MILLER, *Manager*. "Of course not," he said. "Anyone would have noticed that something was wrong."

"You mean he took the room for the express purpose of dying? You saw him once, and never again?"

"I suppose he might . . . no, wait." The manager thought deeply. "No. He registered on a Thursday. I noticed the Belter tan, of course. Then on Friday he went out. I happened to see him pass."

"Was that the day he got the droud? No, skip it, you wouldn't know that. Was it the last time you saw him go out?"

"Yes, it was."

"Then he could have had visitors late Thursday or early Friday."

The manager shook his head, very positively.

"Why not?"

"You see, Mr., uh . . ."

"Hamilton."

"We have a holo camera on every floor, Mr. Hamilton. It takes a picture of each tenant the first time he goes to his room, and then never again. Privacy is one of the services a tenant buys with his room." The manager drew himself up a little as he said this. "For the same reason, the holo camera takes a picture of anyone who is *not* a tenant. The tenants are thus protected from unwarranted intrusions."

"And there were no visitors to any of the rooms on Owen's floor?"

"No, sir, there were not."

"Your tenants are a solitary bunch."

"Perhaps they are."

"I suppose a computer in the basement decides who is and is not a tenant."

"Of course."

"So for six weeks Owen Jennison sat alone in his room. In all that time he was totally ignored."

Miller tried to turn his voice cold, but he was too nervous. "We try to give our guests privacy. If Mr. Jennison had wanted help of any kind he had only to pick up the house phone. He could have called me, or the pharmacy, or the supermarket downstairs."

"Well, thank you, Mr. Miller. That's all I wanted to know. I wanted to know how Owen Jennison could wait six weeks to die while nobody noticed."

Miller swallowed. "He was dying all that time?"

"Yah."

"We had no way of knowing. How could we? I don't see how you can blame us."

"I don't either," I said, and brushed by. Miller had

been close enough, so I had lashed out at him. Now I was ashamed. The man was perfectly right. Owen could have had help it he'd wanted it.

I stood outside, looking up at the jagged blue line of sky that showed between the tops of the buildings. A taxi floated into view, and I beeped my clicker at it, and it dropped.

I went back to ARM Headquarters. Not to work—I couldn't have done any work, not under the circumstances—but to talk to Julie.

Julie. A tall girl, pushing thirty, with green eyes and long hair streaked red and gold. And two wide brown forceps marks above her right knee; but they weren't showing now. I looked into her office, through the one-way glass, and watched her at work.

She sat in a contour couch, smoking. Her eyes were closed. Sometimes her brow would furrow as she concentrated. Sometimes she would snatch a glance at the clock, then close her eyes again.

I didn't interrupt her. I knew the importance of what she was doing.

Julie. She wasn't beautiful. Her eyes were a little too far apart, her chin too square, her mouth too wide. It didn't matter. Because Julie could read minds.

She was the ideal date. She was everything a man needed. A year ago, the day after the night I killed my first man, I had been in a terribly destructive mood. Somehow Julie had turned it into a mood of manic exhilaration. We'd run wild through a supervised anarchy park, running up an enormous bill. We'd hiked five miles without going anywhere, facing backward on a downtown slidewalk. At the end we'd been utterly fatigued, too tired to think . . . But two weeks ago it had been a warm, cuddly, comfortable night. Two people happy with each other; no more than that. Julie was what you needed, anytime, anywhere.

Her male harem must have been the largest in history. To pick up on the thoughts of a male ARM, Julie had to be in love with him. Luckily there was room in her for a lot of love. She didn't demand that we be faithful. A good half of us were married. But there had to be love for each of Julie's men, or Julie couldn't protect him.

She was protecting us now. Each fifteen minutes, Julie was making contact with a specific ARM agent. Psi powers are notoriously undependable, but Julie was an exception. If we got in a hole, Julie was always there to get us out . . . provided some idiot didn't interrupt her at work.

So I stood outside, waiting, with a cigarette in my imaginary hand.

The cigarette was for practice, to stretch the mental muscles. In its way my "hand" was as dependable as Julie's mind-touch, possibly because of its very limitations. Doubt your psi powers and they're gone. A rigidly defined third arm was more reasonable than some warlock ability to make objects move by wishing at them. I knew how an arm felt, and what it would do.

Why do I spend so much time lifting cigarettes? Well, it's the biggest weight I can lift without strain. And there's another reason . . . something taught me by Owen.

At ten minutes to fifteen Julie opened her eyes, rolled out of the contour couch, and came to the door. "Hi, Gil," she said sleepily. "Trouble?"

"Yah. A friend of mine just died. I thought you'd better know." I handed her a cup of coffee.

She nodded. We had a date tonight, and this would change its character. Knowing that, she probed lightly.

"Jesus!" she said, recoiling. "How . . . how horrible. I'm terribly sorry, Gil. Date's off, right?"

"Unless you want to join the ceremonial drunk."

She shook her head vigorously. "I didn't know him. It wouldn't be proper. Besides, you'll be wallowing in your own memories, Gil. A lot of them will be private. I'd cramp your style if you knew I was there to probe. Now if Homer Chandrasekhar were here, it'd be different."

"I wish he were. He'll have to throw his own drunk. Maybe with some of Owen's girls, if they're around."

"You know what I feel," she said.

"Just what I do."

"I wish I could help."

"You always help." I glanced at the clock. "Your coffee break's about over."

"Slave driver." Julie took my earlobe between thumb and forefinger. "Do him proud," she said, and went back to her soundproof room.

She always helps. She doesn't even have to speak. Just knowing that Julie has read my thoughts, that someone understands . . . that's enough.

All alone at three in the afternoon, I started my ceremonial drunk.

The ceremonial drunk is a young custom, not yet tied down by formality. There is no set duration. No specific toasts must be given. Those who participate must be close friends of the deceased, but there is no set number of participants.

I started at the Luau, a place of cool blue light and running water. Outside it was fifteen-thirty in the afternoon, but inside it was evening in the Hawaiian Islands of centuries ago. Already the place was half full. I picked a corner table with considerable elbow room and dialed for Luau grog. It came, cold, brown, and alcoholic, its straw tucked into a cone of ice.

There had been three of us at Cubes Forsythe's ceremonial drunk, one black Ceres night four years ago. A jolly group we were, too; Owen and me and the widow of our third crewman. Gwen Forsythe blamed us for her husband's death. I was just out of the hospital with a right arm that ended at the shoulder, and I blamed Cubes and Owen and myself, all at once. Even Owen had turned dour and introspective. We couldn't have picked a worse trio, or a worse night for it.

But custom called, and we were there. Then as now, I found myself probing my own personality for the wound that was a missing crewman, a missing friend. Introspecting.

Gilbert Hamilton. Born of flatlander parents, in April, 2093, in Topeka, Kansas. Born with two arms and no sign of wild talents.

Flatlander: a Belter term referring to Earthmen, and particularly to Earthmen who had never seen space. I'm not sure my parents ever looked at the stars. They managed the third largest farm in Kansas, ten square miles of arable land between two wide strips of city paralleling two strips of turnpike. We were city people, like all flatlanders, but when the crowds got to be too much for my brothers and me, we had vast stretches of land to be alone in. Ten square miles of playground, with nothing to hamper us but the crops and automachinery.

We looked at the stars, my brothers and I. You can't see stars from the city; the lights hide them. Even in the fields you couldn't see them around the lighted horizon. But straight overhead, they were there: black sky scattered with bright dots, and sometimes a flat white moon.

At twenty I gave up my UN citizenship to become a Belter. I wanted stars, and the Belt government holds title to most of the solar system. There are fabulous riches in the rocks, riches belonging to a scattered civilization of a few hundred thousand Belters; and I wanted my share of that, too.

It wasn't easy. I wouldn't be eligible for a singleship license for ten years. Meanwhile I would be working for others, and learning to avoid mistakes before they killed me. Half the flatlanders who join the Belt die in space before they can earn their licenses.

I mined tin on Mercury and exotic chemicals from Jupiter's atmosphere. I hauled ice from Saturn's rings and quicksilver from Europa. One year our pilot made a mistake pulling up to a new rock, and we damn near had to walk home. Cubes Forsythe was with us then. He managed to fix the com laser and aim it at Icarus to bring us help. Another time the mechanic who did the maintenance job on our ship forgot to replace an absorber, and we all got roaring drunk on the alcohol that built up in our breathing-air. The three of us caught the mechanic six months later. I hear he lived.

Most of the time I was part of a three-man crew. The members changed constantly. When Owen Jennison joined us he replaced a man who had finally earned his singleship license, and couldn't wait to start hunting rocks on his own. He was too eager. I learned later that he'd made one round trip and half of another.

Owen was my age, but more experienced, a Belter born and bred. His blue eyes and blond cockatoo's crest were startling against the dark of his Belter tan, the tan that ended so abruptly where his neck ring cut off the space-intense sunlight his helmet let through. He was permanently chubby, but in free fall it was as if he'd been born with wings. I took to copying his way of moving, much to Cubes' amusement.

I didn't make my own mistake until I was twenty-six.

We were using bombs to put a rock in a new orbit. A contract job. The technique is older than fusion drives, as old as early Belt colonization, and it's still cheaper and faster than using a ship's drive to tow the rock. You use industrial fusion bombs, small and clean, and you set them so that each explosion deepens the crater to channel the force of later blasts.

We'd set four blasts already, four white fireballs that swelled and faded as they rose. When the fifth blast went off we were hovering nearby on the other side of the rock.

The fifth blast shattered the rock.

Cubes had set the bomb. My own mistake was a shared one, because any of the three of us should have had the sense to take off right then. Instead, we watched, cursing, as valuable oxygen-bearing rock became near-valueless shards. We watched the shards spread slowly into a cloud . . . and while we watched, one fast-moving shard reached us. Moving too slowly to vaporize when it hit, it nonetheless sheared through a triple crystal-iron hull, slashed through my upper arm, and pinned Cubes Forsythe to a wall by his heart.

A couple of nudists came in. They stood blinking among the booths while their eyes adjusted to the blue twilight, then converged with glad cries on the group two tables over. I watched and listened with an eye and an ear, thinking how different flatlander nudists were from Belter nudists. These all looked alike. They all had muscles, they had no interesting scars, they carried their credit cards in identical shoulder pouches, and they all shaved the same areas.

. . . We always went nudist in the big bases. Most people did. It was a natural reaction to the pressure suits we wore day and night while out in the rocks. Get him into a shirtsleeve environment, and your normal Belter sneers at a shirt. But it's only for comfort. Give him a good reason and your Belter will don shirt and pants as quickly as the next guy.

But not Owen. After he got that meteor scar, I never

saw him wear a shirt. Not just in the Ceres domes, but anywhere there was air to breathe. He just had to show that scar.

A cool blue mood settled on me, and I remembered . . .

. . . Owen Jennison lounging on a corner of my hospital bed, telling me of the trip back. I couldn't remember anything after that rock had sheared through my arm.

I should have bled to death in seconds. Owen hadn't given me the chance. The wound was ragged; Owen had sliced it clean to the shoulder with one swipe of a com laser. Then he'd tied a length of fiberglass curtain over the flat surface and knotted it tight under my remaining armpit. He told me about putting me under two atmospheres of pure oxygen as a substitute for replacing the blood I'd lost. He told me how he'd reset the fusion drive for four gees to get me back in time. By rights we should have gone up in a cloud of starfire and glory.

"So there goes my reputation. The whole Belt knows how I rewired our drive. A lot of 'em figure if I'm stupid enough to risk my own life like that, I'd risk theirs too."

"So you're not safe to travel with."

"Just so. They're starting to call me Four Gee Jennison."

"You think you've got problems? I can just see how it'll be when I get out of this bed. 'You do something stupid, Gil?' The hell of it is, it *was* stupid."

"So lie a little."

"Uh huh. Can we sell the ship?"

"Nope. Gwen inherited a third interest in it from Cubes. She won't sell."

"Then we're effectively broke."

"Except for the ship. We need another crewman."

"Correction. *You* need *two* crewmen. Unless you want to fly with a one-armed man. I can't afford a transplant."

Owen hadn't tried to offer me a loan. That would have been insulting, even if he'd had the money. "What's wrong with a prosthetic?"

"An iron arm? Sorry, no. I'm squeamish."

Owen had looked at me strangely, but all he'd said

was, "Well, we'll wait a bit. Maybe you'll change your mind."

He hadn't pressured me. Not then, and not later, after I'd left the hospital and taken an apartment while I waited to get used to a missing arm. If he thought I would eventually settle for a prosthetic, he was mistaken.

Why? It's not a question I can answer. Others obviously feel differently; there are millions of people walking around with metal and plastic and silicone parts. Part man, part machine, and how do they themselves know which is the real person?

I'd rather be dead than part metal. Call it a quirk. Call it, even, the same quirk that makes my skin crawl when I find a place like Monica Apartments. A human being should be all human. He should have habits and possessions peculiarly his own, he should not try to look like or to behave like anyone but himself, and he should not be half robot.

So there I was, Gil the Arm, learning to eat with my left hand.

An amputee never entirely loses what he's lost. My missing fingers itched. I moved to keep from barking my missing elbow on sharp corners. I reached for things, then swore when they didn't come.

Owen had hung around, though his own emergency funds must have been running low. I hadn't offered to sell my third of the ship, and he hadn't asked.

There had been a girl. Now I'd forgotten her name. One night I was at her place waiting for her to get dressed—a dinner date—and I'd happened to see a nail file she'd left on a table. I'd picked it up. I'd almost tried to file my nails, but remembered in time. Irritated, I had tossed the file back on the table—and missed.

Like an idiot I'd tried to catch it with my right hand.

And I'd caught it.

I'd never suspected myself of having psychic powers. You have to be in the right frame of mind to use a psi power. But who had ever had a better opportunity than I did that night, with a whole section of brain tuned to the nerves and muscles of my right arm, and no right arm?

I'd held the nail file in my imaginary hand. I'd felt it, just as I'd felt my missing fingernails getting too long. I had run my thumb along the rough steel surface; I had turned the file in my fingers. Telekinesis for lift, esper for touch.

"That's it," Owen had said the next day. "That's all we need. One crewman, and you with your eldritch powers. You practice, see how strong you can get that lift. I'll go find a sucker."

"He'll have to settle for a sixth of net. Cubes' widow will want her share."

"Don't worry. I'll swing it."

"Don't worry!" I'd waved a pencil stub at him. Even in Ceres' gentle gravity, it was as much as I could lift— then. "You don't think TK and esper can make do for a real arm, do you?"

"It's better than a real arm. You'll see. You'll be able to reach through your suit with it without losing pressure. What Belter can do that?"

"Sure."

"What the hell do you want, Gil? Someone should give you your arm back? You can't have that. You lost it fair and square, through stupidity. Now it's your choice. Do you fly with an imaginary arm, or do you go back to Earth?"

"I can't go back. I don't have the fare."

"Well?"

"Okay, okay. Go find us a crewman. Someone I can impress with my imaginary arm."

I sucked meditatively on a second Luau grog. By now all the booths were full, and a second layer was forming around the bar. The voices made a continuous hypnotic roar. Cocktail hour had arrived.

. . . He'd swung it, all right. On the strength of my imaginary arm, Owen had talked a kid named Homer Chandrasekhar into joining our crew.

He'd been right about my arm, too.

Others with similar senses can reach further, up to halfway around the world. My unfortunately literal imagination had restricted me to a psychic hand. But my esper fingertips were more sensitive, more dependable. I could lift more weight. Today, in Earth's gravity, I can lift a full shot glass.

I found I could reach through a cabin wall to feel for

breaks in the circuits behind it. In vacuum I could brush dust from the outside of my faceplate. In port I did magic tricks.

I'd almost ceased to feel like a cripple. It was all due to Owen. In six months of mining I had paid off my hospital bills and earned my fare back to Earth, with a comfortable stake left over.

"Finagle's Black Humor!" Owen had exploded when I told him. "Of all places, why Earth?"

"Because if I can get my UN citizenship back, Earth will replace my arm. Free."

"Oh. That's true," he'd said dubiously.

The Belt had organ banks too, but they were always undersupplied. Belters didn't give things away. Neither did the Belt government. They kept the prices on transplants as high as they would go. Thus they dropped the demand to meet the supply, and kept taxes down to boot.

In the Belt I'd have to buy my own arm. And I didn't have the money. On Earth there was social security, and a vast supply of transplant material.

What Owen had said couldn't be done, I'd done. I'd found someone to hand me my arm back.

Sometimes I'd wondered if Owen held the choice against me. He'd never said anything, but Homer Chandrasekhar had spoken at length. A Belter would have earned his arm or done without. Never would he have accepted charity.

Was that why Owen hadn't tried to call me?

I shook my head. I didn't believe it.

The room continued to lurch after my head stopped shaking. I'd had enough for the moment. I finished my third grog and ordered dinner.

Dinner sobered me for the next lap. It was something of a shock to realize that I'd run through the entire lifespan of my friendship with Owen Jennison. I'd known him for three years, though it had seemed like half a lifetime. And it was. Half my six-year lifespan as a Belter.

I ordered coffee grog and watched the man pour it: hot, milky coffee laced with cinnamon and other spices, and high-proof rum poured in a stream of blue fire. This was one of the special drinks served by a human headwaiter, and it was the reason they kept him around. Phase two of the ceremonial drunk: blow half your fortune, in the grand manner.

But I called Ordaz before I touched the drink.

"Yes, Mr. Hamilton? I was just going home for dinner."

"I won't keep you long. Have you found out anything new?"

Ordaz took a closer look at my phone image. His disapproval was plain. "I see that you have been drinking. Perhaps you should go home now, and call me tomorrow."

I was shocked. "Don't you know *anything* about Belt customs?"

"I do not understand."

I explained the ceremonial drunk. "Look, Ordaz, if you know that little about the way a Belter thinks, then we'd better have a talk. Soon. Otherwise you're likely to miss something."

"You may be right. I can see you at noon, over lunch."

"Good. What have you got?"

"Considerable, but none of it is very helpful. Your friend landed on Earth two months ago, arriving on the *Pillar of Fire*, operating out of Outback Field, Australia. He was wearing a haircut in the style of Earth. From there—"

"That's funny. He'd have had to wait two months for his hair to grow out."

"That occurred even to me. I understand that a Belter commonly shaves his entire scalp, except for a strip two inches wide running from the nape of his neck forward."

"The strip cut, yah. It probably started when someone decided he'd live longer if his hair couldn't fall in his eyes during a tricky landing. But Owen could have let his hair grow out during a singleship mining trip. There'd be nobody to see."

"Still, it seems odd. Did you know that Mr. Jennison has a cousin on Earth? One Harvey Peele, who manages a chain of supermarkets."

"So I wasn't his next of kin, even on Earth."

"Mr. Jennison made no attempt to contact him."

"Anything else?"

"I've spoken to the man who sold Mr. Jennison his droud and plug. Kenneth Graham owns an office and operating room on Gayley in Near West Los Angeles. Graham claims that the droud was a standard type, that your friend must have altered it himself."

"Do you believe him?"

"For the present. His permits and his records are all in order. The droud was altered with a soldering iron, an amateur's tool."

"Uh huh."

"As far as the police are concerned, the case will probably be closed when we locate the tools Mr. Jennison used."

"Tell you what. I'll wire Homer Chandrasekhar tomorrow. Maybe he can find out things—why Owen landed without a strip haircut, why he came to Earth at all."

Ordaz shrugged with his eyebrows. He thanked me for my trouble and hung up.

The coffee grog was still hot. I gulped at it, savoring the sugary, bittery sting of it, trying to forget Owen dead and remember him in life. He was always slightly chubby, I remembered, but he never gained a pound and he never lost a pound. He could move like a whippet when he had to.

And now he was terribly thin, and his death-grin was ripe with obscene joy.

I ordered another coffee grog. The waiter, a showman, made sure he had my attention before he lit the heated rum, then poured it from a foot above the glass. You can't drink that drink slowly. It slides down too easily, and there's the added spur that if you wait too long it might get cold. Rum and strong coffee. Two of these and I'd be drunkenly alert for hours.

Midnight found me in the Mars Bar, running on scotch and soda. In between I'd been barhopping. Irish coffee at Bergin's, cold and smoking concoctions at the Moon Pool, scotch and wild music at Beyond. I couldn't get drunk, and I couldn't find the right mood. There was a barrier to the picture I was trying to rebuild.

It was the memory of the last Owen, grinning in an armchair with a wire leading down into his brain.

I didn't know that Owen. I had never met the man, and never would have wanted to. From bar to nightclub to restaurant I had run from the image, waiting for the alcohol to break the barrier between present and past.

So I sat at a corner table, surrounded by 3D panoramic views of an impossible Mars. Crystal towers and long, straight blue canali, six-legged beasts and beautiful, impossibly slender men and women, looked out at me across never-never land. Would Owen have found it sad or funny? He'd seen the real Mars, and had not been impressed.

I had reached that stage where time becomes discontinuous, where gaps of seconds or minutes appear between the events you can remember. Somewhere in that period I found myself staring at a cigarette. I must have just lighted it, because it was near its original two-hundred-millimeter length. Maybe a waiter had snuck up behind me. There it was, at any rate, burning between my middle and index fingers.

I stared at the coal as the mood settled on me. I was calm, I was drifting, I was lost in time . . .

. . . We'd been two months in the rocks, our first trip out since the accident. Back we came to Ceres with a holdful of gold, fifty percent pure, guaranteed suitable for rustproof wiring and conductor plates. At nightfall we were ready to celebrate.

We walked along the city limits, with neon blinking and beckoning on the right, a melted rock cliff to the left, and stars blazing through the dome overhead. Homer Chandrasekhar was practically snorting. On this night his first trip out culminated in his first homecoming: and homecoming is the best part.

"We'll want to split up about midnight," he said. He didn't need to enlarge on that. Three men in company might conceivably be three singleship pilots, but chances are they're a ship's crew. They don't have their singleship licenses yet; they're too stupid or too inexperienced. If we wanted companions for the night—

"You haven't thought this through," Owen answered. I saw Homer's double take, then his quick look at where my shoulder ended, and I was ashamed. I didn't need my crewmates to hold my hand, and in this state I'd only slow them down.

Before I could open my mouth to protest, Owen went on. "Think it through. We've got a draw here that we'd be idiots to throw away. Gil, pick up a cigarette. No, not with your left hand—"

I was drunk, gloriously drunk and feeling immortal. The attenuated Martians seemed to move in the walls, the walls that seemed to be picture windows on a Mars that never was. For the first time that night, I raised my glass in toast.

"To Owen, from Gil the Arm. Thanks."

I transferred the cigarette to my imaginary hand.

By now you've got the idea I was holding it in my imaginary fingers. Most people have the same impression, but it isn't so. I held it clutched ignominiously in my fist. The coal couldn't burn me, of course, but it still felt like a lead ingot.

I rested my imaginary elbow on the table, and that seemed to make it easier—which is ridiculous, but it works. Truly, I'd expected my imaginary arm to disappear after I got the transplant. But I'd found I could dissociate from the new arm to hold small objects in my invisible hand, to feel tactile sensations in my invisible fingertips.

I'd earned the title Gil the Arm, that night in Ceres. It had started with a floating cigarette. Owen had been right. Everyone in the place eventually wound up staring at the floating cigarette smoked by the one-armed man. All I had to do was find the prettiest girl in the room with my peripheral vision, then catch her eye.

That night we had been the center of the biggest impromptu party ever thrown in Ceres Base. It wasn't planned that way at all. I'd used the cigarette trick three times, so that each of us would have a date. But the third girl already had an escort, and he was celebrating something; he'd sold some kind of patent to an Earth-based industrial firm. He was throwing money around like confetti. So we let him stay. I did tricks, reaching esper fingers into a closed box to tell what was inside, and by the time I finished all the tables had been pushed together and I was in the center, with Homer and Owen and three girls. Then we got to singing old songs, and the bartenders joined us, and suddenly everything was on the house.

Eventually about twenty of us wound up in the orbiting mansion of the First Speaker for the Belt Government. The goldskin cops had tried to bust us up earlier, and the First Speaker had behaved very rudely indeed, then compensated by inviting them to join us . . .

And that was why I used TK on so many cigarettes.

Across the width of the Mars Bar, a girl in a peach-colored dress sat studying me with her chin on her fist. I got up and went over.

My head felt fine. It was the first thing I checked when I woke up. Apparently I'd remembered to take a hangover pill.

A leg was hooked over my knee. It felt good, though the pressure had put my foot to sleep. Fragrant dark hair spilled beneath my nose. I didn't move. I didn't want her to know I was awake.

It's damned embarrassing when you wake up with a girl and can't remember her name.

Well, let's see. A peach dress neatly hung from a doorknob . . . I remembered a whole lot of traveling last night. The girl at the Mars Bar. A puppet show. Music of all kinds. I'd talked about Owen, and she'd steered me away from that because it depressed her. Then—

Hah! Taffy. Last name forgotten.

"Morning," I said.

"Morning," she said. "Don't try to move, we're hooked together . . ." In the sober morning light she was lovely. Long black hair, brown eyes, creamy untanned skin. To be lovely this early was a neat trick, and I told her so, and she smiled.

My lower leg was dead meat until it started to buzz with renewed circulation, and then I made faces until it calmed down. Taffy kept up a running chatter as we dressed. "That third hand is strange. I remember you holding me with two strong arms and stroking the back of my neck with the third. *Very* nice. It reminded me of a Fritz Leiber story."

"*The Wanderer*. The panther girl."

"Mm hmm. How many girls have you caught with that cigarette trick?"

"None as pretty as you."

"And how many girls have you told that to?"

"Can't remember. It always worked before. Maybe this time it's for real."

We exchanged grins.

A minute later I caught her frowning thoughtfully at the back of my neck. "Something wrong?"

"I was just thinking. You really crashed and burned last night. I hope you don't drink that much all the time."

"Why? You worried about me?"

She blushed, then nodded.

"I should have told you. In fact, I think I did, last night. I was on a ceremonial drunk. When a good friend dies it's obligatory to get smashed."

Taffy looked relieved. "I didn't mean to get—"

"Personal? Why not. You've the right. Anyway, I like —" *maternal types*, but I couldn't say that. "People who worry about me."

Taffy touched her hair with some kind of complex comb. A few strokes snapped her hair instantly into place. Static electricity?

"It was a good drunk," I said. "Owen would have been proud. And that's all the mourning I'll do. One drunk and—" I spread my hands. "Out."

"It's not a bad way to go," Taffy mused reflectively. "Current stimulus, I mean. I mean, if you've got to bow out—"

"Now drop that!" I don't know how I got so angry so fast. Ghoul-thin and grinning in a reading chair, Owen's corpse was suddenly vivid before me. I'd fought that image for too many hours. "Walking off a bridge is enough of a cop-out," I snarled. "Dying for a month while current burns out your brain is nothing less than sickening."

Taffy was hurt and bewildered. "But your friend did it, didn't he? You didn't make him sound like a weakling."

"Nuts," I heard myself say. "He didn't do it. He was—"

Just like that, I was sure. I must have realized it while I was drunk or sleeping. Of *course* he hadn't killed himself. *That* wasn't Owen. And current addiction wasn't Owen either.

"He was murdered," I said. "Sure he was. Why didn't I see it?" And I made a dive for the phone.

"Good morning, Mr. Hamilton." Detective-Inspector Ordaz looked very fresh and neat this morning. I was suddenly aware that I hadn't shaved. "I see you remembered to take your hangover pills."

"Right. Ordaz, has it occurred to you that Owen might have been murdered?"

"Naturally. But it isn't possible."

"I think it might be. Suppose he—"

"Mr. Hamilton."

"Yah?"

"We have an appointment for lunch. Shall we discuss it then? Meet me at Headquarters at twelve hundred."

"Okay. One thing you might take care of this morning. See if Owen registered for a nudist's license."

"Do you think he might have?"

"Yah. I'll tell you why at lunch."

"Very well."

"Don't hang up. You said you'd found the man who sold Owen his droud-and-plug. What was his name again?"

"Kenneth Graham."

"That's what I thought." I hung up.

Taffy touched my shoulder. "Do—do you really think he might have been—killed?"

"Yah. The whole setup depended on him not being able to—"

"No. Wait. I don't want to know about it."

I turned to look at her. She really didn't. The very subject of a stranger's death was making her sick to her stomach.

"Okay. Look, I'm a jerk not to at least offer you breakfast, but I've got to get on this right away. Can I call you a cab?"

When the cab came I dropped a ten-mark coin in the slot and helped her in. I got her address before it took off.

ARM Headquarters hummed with early morning activity. Hellos came my way, and I answered them without stopping to talk. Anything important would filter down to me eventually.

As I passed Julie's cubicle I glanced in. She was hard at work, limply settled in her contour couch, jotting notes with her eyes closed.

Kenneth Graham.

A hookup to the basement computer formed the greater part of my desk. Learning how to use it had taken me several months. I typed an order for coffee and donuts, then: INFORMATION RETRIEVAL. KENNETH GRAHAM. LIMITED LICENSE: SURGERY. GENERAL LICENSE: DIRECT CURRENT STIMULUS EQUIPMENT SALES. ADDRESS: NEAR WEST LOS ANGELES.

Tape chattered out of the slot, an instant response, loop after loop of it curling on my desk. I didn't need to read it to know I was right.

New technologies create new customs, new laws, new ethics, new crimes. About half the activity of the United Nations Police, the ARMs, dealt with control of a crime that hadn't existed a century ago. The crime of organlegging was the result of thousands of years of medical progress, of millions of lives selflessly dedicated to the ideal of healing the sick. Progress had brought these ideals to reality, and, as usual, had created new problems.

1900 A.D. was the year Karl Landsteiner classified human blood into four types, giving patients their first real chance to survive a transfusion. The technology of transplants had grown with the growing of the twentieth century. Whole blood, dry bone, skin, live kidneys, live hearts could all be transfered from one body to another. Donors had saved tens of thousands of lives in that hundred years, by willing their bodies to medicine.

But the number of donors was limited, and not many died in such a way that anything of value could be saved.

The deluge had come something less than a hundred years ago. One healthy donor (but of course there was no such animal) could save a dozen lives. Why, then, should a condemned murderer die to no purpose? First a few states, then most of the nations of the world had passed new laws. Criminals condemned to death must be executed in a hospital, with surgeons to save as much as could be saved for the organ banks.

The world's billions wanted to live, and the organ banks were life itself. A man could live forever as long as the doctors could shove spare parts into him faster than his own parts wore out. But they could do that only as long as the world's organ banks were stocked.

A hundred scattered movements to abolish the death penalty died silent, unpublicized deaths. Everybody gets sick sometime.

And still there were shortages in the organ banks. Still patients died for the lack of parts to save them. The world's legislators had responded to steady pressure from the world's people. Death penalties were established for first, second, and third degree murder. For assault with a deadly weapon. Then for a multitude of crimes: rape, fraud, embezzlement, having children without a license, four or more counts of false advertising. For nearly a century the trend had been growing, as the world's voting citizens acted to protect their right to live forever.

Even now there weren't enough transplants. A woman with kidney trouble might wait a year for a transplant: one healthy kidney to last the rest of her life. A thirty-five-year-old heart patient must live with a sound but forty-year-old heart. One lung, part of a liver, prosthetics that wore out too fast or weighed too much or did too little . . . there weren't enough criminals. Not surprisingly, the death penalty *was* a deterrent. People stopped committing crimes rather than face the donor room of a hospital.

For instant replacement of your ruined digestive system, for a *young* healthy heart, for a whole liver when you'd ruined yours with alcohol . . . you had to go to an organlegger.

There are three aspects to the business of organlegging.

One is the business of kidnap-murder. It's risky. You can't fill an organ bank by waiting for volunteers. Executing condemned criminals is a government monopoly. So you go out and *get* your donors: on a crowded city slidewalk, in an air terminal, stranded on a freeway by a car with a busted capacitor . . . anywhere.

The selling end of the business is just as dangerous, because even a desperately sick man sometimes has a conscience. He'll buy his transplant, then go straight to the ARMs, curing his sickness and his conscience by turning in the whole gang. Thus the sales end is somewhat anonymous, but as there are few repeat sales, that hardly matters.

Third is the technical, medical aspect. Probably this is the safest part of the business. Your hospital is big, but you can put it anywhere. You wait for the donors, who arrive still alive; you ship out livers and glands and square feet of live skin, correctly labeled for rejection reactions.

It's not as easy as it sounds. You need doctors. Good ones.

That was where Loren came in. He had a monopoly.

Where did he get them? We were still trying to find out. Somehow, one man had discovered a foolproof way to recruit talented but dishonest doctors practically en masse. Was it really one man? All our sources said it was. And he had half the North American west coast in the palm of his hand.

Loren. No holographs, no fingerprints or retina prints, not even a description. All we had was that one name, and a few possible contacts.

One of these was Kenneth Graham.

The holograph was a good one. Probably it had been posed in a portrait shop. Kenneth Graham had a long Scottish face with a lantern jaw and a small, dour mouth. In the holo he was trying to smile and look dignified simultaneously. He only looked uncomfortable. His hair was sandy and close cut. Above his light gray eyes his eyebrows were so light as to be nearly invisible.

My breakfast arrived. I dunked a donut and bit it, and found out I was hungrier than I'd thought.

A string of holos had been reproduced on the computer tape. I ran through the others fairly quickly, eating with one hand and flipping the key with the other. Some were fuzzy; they had been taken by spy beams through the windows of Graham's shop. None of the prints were in any way incriminating. Not one showed Graham smiling.

He had been selling electrical joy for twelve years now.

A current addict has an advantage over his supplier. Electricity is cheap. With a drug, your supplier can always raise the price on you; but not with electricity. You see the ecstasy merchant once, when he sells you your operation and your droud, and never again. Nobody gets hooked by accident. There's an honesty to current addiction. The customer always knows just what he's getting into, and what it will do for him—and to him.

Still, you'd need a certain lack of empathy to make a living the way Kenneth Graham did. Else he'd have had to turn away his customers. Nobody becomes a current addict gradually. He decides all at once, and he buys the operation before he has ever tasted its joy. Each of Kenneth Graham's customers had reached his shop after deciding to drop out of the human race.

What a stream of the hopeless and the desperate must have passed through Graham's shop! How could they help but haunt his dreams? And if Kenneth Graham slept well at night, then—

Then, small wonder if he had turned organlegger.

He was in a good position for it. Despair is characteristic of the would-be current addict. The unknown, the unloved, the people nobody knew and nobody needed and nobody missed, these passed in a steady stream through Kenneth Graham's shop.

So a few didn't come out. Who'd notice?

I flipped quickly through the tape to find out who was in charge of watching Graham. Jackson Bera. I called down through the desk phone.

"Sure," said Bera, "we've had a spy beam on him about three weeks now. It's a waste of good salaried ARM agents. Maybe he's clean. Maybe he's been tipped somehow."

"Then why not stop watching him?"

Bera looked disgusted. "Because we've only been watching for three weeks. How many donors do you think he needs a year? Two. Read the reports. Gross profit on a single donor is over a million UN marks. Graham can afford to be careful who he picks."

"Yah."

"At that, he wasn't careful enough. At least two of his customers disappeared last year. Customers with families. That's what put us on him."

"So you could watch him for the next six months without a guarantee. He could be just waiting for the right guy to walk in."

"Sure. He has to write up a report on every customer. That gives him the right to ask personal questions. If the guy has relatives, Graham lets him walk out. Most people do have relatives, you know. Then again," Bera said disconsolately, "he could be clean. Sometimes a current addict disappears without help."

"How come I didn't see any holos of Graham at home? You can't be watching just his shop."

Jackson Bera scratched at his hair. Hair like black steel wool, worn long like a bushman's mop. "Sure we're watching his place, but we can't get a spy beam in there. It's an inside apartment. No windows. You know anything about spy beams?"

"Not much. I know they've been around awhile."

"They're as old as lasers. Oldest trick in the book is to put a mirror in the room you want to bug. Then you run a laser beam through a window, or even through heavy drapes, and bounce it off the mirror. When you pick it up it's been distorted by the vibrations in the glass. That gives you a perfect recording of anything that's been said in that room. But for pictures you need something a little more sophisticated."

"How sophisticated can we get?"

"We can put a spy beam in any room with a window. We can send one through some kinds of wall. Give us an optically flat surface and we can send one around corners."

"But you need an outside wall."

"Yup."

"What's Graham doing now?"

"Just a sec." Bera disappeared from view. "Someone just came in. Graham's talking to him. Want the picture?"

"Sure. Leave it on. I'll turn it off from here when I'm through with it."

The picture of Bera went dark. A moment later I was looking into a doctor's office. If I'd seen it cold I'd have thought it was run by a podiatrist. There was the comfortable tilt-back chair with the headrest and the footrest; the cabinet next to it with instruments lying on top, on a clean white cloth; the desk over in one corner. Kenneth Graham was talking to a homely, washed-out-looking girl.

I listened to Graham's would-be-fatherly reassurances and his glowing description of the magic of current addicition. When I couldn't take it any longer I turned the sound down. The girl took her place in the chair, and Graham placed something over her head.

The girl's homely face turned suddenly beautiful.

Happiness is beautiful, all by itself. A happy person is beautiful, per se. Suddenly and totally, the girl was full of joy and I realized that I hadn't known everything about droud sales. Apparently Graham had an inductor to put the current where he wanted it, without wires. He *could* show a customer what current addiction felt like, without first implanting the wires.

What a powerful argument that was!

Graham turned off the machine. It was as if he'd turned off the girl. She sat stunned for a moment, then reached frantically for her purse and started scrabbling inside.

I couldn't take anymore. I turned it off.

Small wonder if Graham had turned organlegger. He had to be totally without empathy just to sell his merchandise.

Even there, I thought, he'd had a head start.

So he was a little more callous than the rest of the world's billions. But not much. Every voter had a bit of the organlegger in him. In voting the death penalty for so many crimes, the law makers had only bent to pressure from the voters. There was a spreading lack of respect for life, the evil side of transplant technology. The good side was a longer life for everyone. One condemned criminal could save a dozen deserving lives. Who could complain about that?

We hadn't thought that way in the Belt. In the Belt survival was a virtue in itself, and life was a precious thing, spread so thin among the sterile rocks, hurtling in single units through all that killing emptiness between the worlds.

So I'd had to come to Earth for my transplant.

My request had been accepted two months after I landed. So quickly? Later I'd learned that the banks always have a surplus of certain items. Few people lose their arms these days. I had also learned, a year after the transplant had taken, that I was using an arm taken from a captured organlegger's storage bank.

That had been a shock. I'd hoped my arm had come from a depraved murderer, someone who'd shot fourteen nurses from a rooftop. Not at all. Some faceless, nameless victim had had the bad luck to encounter a ghoul, and I had benefited thereby.

Did I turn in my new arm in a fit of revulsion? No, surprising to say, I did not. But I had joined the ARMs, once the Amalgamation of Regional Militia, now the United Nations Police. Though I had stolen a dead man's arm, I would hunt the kin of those who had killed him.

The noble urgency of that resolve had been drowned in paperwork these last few years. Perhaps I was becoming callous, like the flatlanders—the *other* flatlanders around me, voting new death penalties year after year. *Income-tax evasion. Operating a flying vehicle on manual controls over a city.*

Was Kenneth Graham so much worse than they?

Sure he was. The bastard had put a wire in Owen Jennison's head.

I waited twenty minutes for Julie to come out. I could have sent her a memorandum, but there was plenty of time before noon, and too little time to get anything accomplished, and . . . I wanted to talk to her.

"Hi," she said. "Thanks," taking the coffee. "How went the ceremonial drunk? Oh, I *see*. Mmmmm. Very good. Almost poetic." Conversation with Julie has a way of taking shortcuts.

Poetic, right. I remembered how inspiration had struck like lightning through a mild high glow. Owen's floating cigarette lure. What better way to honor his memory than to use it to pick up a girl?

"Right," Julie agreed. "But there's something you may have missed. What's Taffy's last name?"

"I can't remember. She wrote it down on—"

"What does she do for a living?"

"How should I know?"

"What religion is she? Is she a pro or an anti? Where did she grow up?"

"Dammit—"

"Half an hour ago you were very complacently musing on how depersonalized all us flatlanders are except you. What's Taffy, a person or a foldout?" Julie stood with her hands on her hips, looking up at me like a short schoolteacher.

How many people is Julie? Some of us have never seen this Guardian aspect. She's frightening, the Guardian. If it ever appeared on a date, the man she was with would be struck impotent forever.

It never does. When a reprimand is deserved, Julie delivers it in broad daylight. This serves to separate her functions, but it doesn't make it easier to take.

No use pretending it wasn't her business, either.

I'd come here to ask for Julie's protection. Let me turn unlovable to Julie, even a little bit unlovable, and as far as Julie was concerned I would have an unreadable mind. How, then, would she know when I was in trouble? How could she send help to rescue me from whatever? My private life *was* her business, her single, vastly important job.

"I *like* Taffy," I protested. "I didn't care who she was when we met. Now I like her, and I think she likes me. What do you want from a first date?"

"You know better. You can remember other dates when two of you talked all night on a couch, just from the joy of learning about each other." She mentioned three names, and I flushed. Julie knows the words that will turn you inside out in an instant. "Taffy is a person, not an episode, not a symbol of anything, not just a pleasant night. What's your judgment of her?"

I thought about it, standing there in the corridor. Funny: I've faced the Guardian Julie on other occasions, and it has never occurred to me to just walk out of the unpleasant siuation. Later I think of that. At the time I just stand there, facing the Guardian/Judge/ Teacher. I thought about Taffy . . .

"She's nice," I said. *"Not* depersonalized. Squeamish, even. She wouldn't make a good nurse. She'd want to help too much, and it would tear her apart when she couldn't. I'd say she was one of the vulnerable ones."

"Go on."

"I want to see her again, but I won't dare talk shop with her. In fact . . . I'd better not see her till this business of Owen is over. Loren might take an interest in her. Or . . . she might take an interest in me, and I might get hurt . . . have I missed anything?"

"I think so. You owe her a phone call. If you won't be dating her for a few days, call her and tell her so."

"Check." I spun on my heel, spun back. "Finagle's Jest! I almost forgot. The reason I came here—"

"I know, you want a time slot. Suppose I check on you at oh nine forty-five every morning?"

"That's a little early. When I get in deadly danger it's usually at night."

"I'm off at night. Oh nine forty-five is all I've got. I'm sorry, Gil, but it is. Shall I monitor you or not?"

"Sold. Nine forty-five."

"Good. Let me know if you get real proof Owen was murdered. I'll give you two slots. You'll be in a little more concrete danger then."

"Good."

"I love you. Yeep, I'm late." And she dodged back into the office, while I went to call Taffy.

Taffy wasn't home, of course, and I didn't know where she worked, or even what she did. Her phone offered to take a message. I gave my name and said I'd call back.

And then I sat there sweating for five minutes.

It was half an hour to noon. Here I was at my desk phone. I couldn't decently see any way to argue myself out of sending a message to Homer Chandrasekhar.

I didn't want to talk to him, then or ever. He'd chewed me out but good, last time I'd seen him. My free arm had cost me my Belter life, and it had cost me Homer's respect. I didn't want to talk to him, even on a one-way message, and I most particularly didn't want to have to tell him Owen was dead.

But someone had to tell him.

And maybe he could find out something.

And I'd put it off nearly a full day.

For five minutes I sweated, and then I called long distance and recorded a message and sent it off to Ceres. More accurately, I recorded six messages before I was satisfied. I don't want to talk about it.

I tried Taffy again; she might come home for lunch. Wrong.

I hung up wondering if Julie had been fair. What had we bargained for, Taffy and I, beyond a pleasant night? And we'd had that, and would have others, with luck.

But Julie would find it hard not to be fair. If she thought Taffy was the vulnerable type, she'd taken her information from my own mind.

Mixed feelings. You're a kid, and your mother has just laid down the law. But it *is* a law, something you can count on . . . and she *is* paying attention to you . . . and she *does* care . . . when, for so many of those outside, nobody cares at all.

"Naturally I thought of murder," said Ordaz. "I always consider murder. When my sainted mother passed away after three years of the most tender care by my sister Maria Angela, I actually considered searching for evidence of needle holes about the head."

"Find any?"

Ordaz' face froze. He put down his beer and started to get up.

"Cool it," I said hurriedly. "No offense intended." He glared a moment, then sat down half mollified.

We'd picked an outdoor restaurant on the pedestrian level. On the other side of a hedge (a real live hedge, green and growing and everything) the shoppers were carried past in a steady one-way stream. Beyond them, a slidewalk carried a similar stream in the opposite direction. I had the dizzy feeling that it was we who were moving.

A waiter like a bell-bottomed chess pawn produced steaming dishes of chili size from its torso, put them precisely in front of us, and slid away on a cushion of air.

"Naturally I considered murder. Believe me. Mr. Hamilton, it does not hold up."

"I think I could make a pretty good case."

"You may try, of course. Better, I will start you on your way. First, we must assume that Kenneth Graham the happiness peddler did not sell a droud-and-plug to Owen Jennison. Rather, Owen Jennison was forced to undergo the operation. Graham's records, including the written permission to operate, were forged. All this we must assume, is it not so?"

"Right. And before you tell me Graham's escutcheon is unblemished, let me tell you that it isn't."

"Oh?"

"He's connected with an organlegging gang. That's classified information. We're watching him, and we don't want him tipped."

"That is news." Ordaz rubbed his jaw. "Organlegging. Well. What would Owen Jennison have to do with organlegging?"

"Owen's a Belter. The Belt's always drastically short of transplant materials."

"Yes, they import quantities of medical supplies from Earth. Not only organs in storage, but also drugs and prosthetics. So?"

"Owen ran a good many cargos past the goldskins in his day. He got caught a few times, but he's still way ahead of the government. He's on the records as a successful smuggler. If a big organlegger wanted to expand his market, he might very well send a feeler out to a Belter with a successful smuggling record."

"You never mentioned that Mr. Jennison was a smuggler."

"What for? All Belters are smugglers, if they think they can get away with it. To a Belter, smuggling isn't immoral. But an organlegger wouldn't know that. He'd think Owen was already a criminal."

"Do you think your friend—" Ordaz hesitated delicately.

"No, Owen wouldn't turn organlegger. But he might, he just *might* try to turn one in. The rewards for information leading to the capture and conviction of, et cetera, are substantial. If someone contracted Owen, Owen might very well have tried to trace the contact by himself.

"Now, the gang we're after covers half the west coast

of this continent. That's big. It's the Loren gang, the one Graham may be working for. Suppose Owen had a chance to meet Loren himself?"

"You think he might take it, do you?"

"I think he did. I think he let his hair grow out so he'd look like an Earthman, to convince Loren he wanted to look inconspicuous. I think he collected as much information as he could, then tried to get out with a whole skin. But he didn't make it.

"Did you find his application for a nudist license?"

"No. I saw your point there," said Ordaz. He leaned back, ignoring the food in front of him. "Mr. Jennison's tan was uniform except for the characteristic darkening of the face. I presume he was a practicing nudist in the Belt."

"Yah. We don't need licenses there. He'd have been one here, too, unless he was hiding something. Remember that scar. He never missed a chance to show it off."

"Could he really have thought to pass for a—" Ordaz hesitated—"flatlander?"

"With that Belter tan? No! He was overdoing it a little with the haircut. Maybe he thought Loren would underestimate him. But he wasn't advertising his presence, or he wouldn't have left his most personal possessions home."

"So he was dealing with organleggers, and they found him out before he could reach you. Yes, Mr. Hamilton, this is well thought out. But it won't work."

"Why not? I'm not trying to prove it's murder. Not yet. I'm just trying to show you that murder is at least as likely as suicide."

"But it's not, Mr. Hamilton."

I looked the question.

"Consider the details of the hypothetical murder. Owen Jennison is drugged, no doubt, and taken to the office of Kenneth Graham. There, an ecstasy plug is attached. A standard droud is fitted, and is then amateurishly altered with soldering tools. Already we see, on the part of the killer, a minute attention to details. We see it again in Kenneth Graham's forged papers of permission to operate. They were impeccable.

"Owen Jennison is then taken back to his apartment. It would be his own, would it not? There would be little point in moving him to another. The cord from his droud is shortened, again in amateurish fashion. Mr. Jennison is tied up—"

"I wondered if you'd see that."

"But why should he not be tied up? He is tied up, and allowed to waken. Perhaps the arrangement is explained to him, perhaps not. That would be up to the killer. The killer then plugs Mr. Jennison into a wall. A current trickles through his brain, and Owen Jennison knows pure pleasure for the first time in his life.

"He is left tied up for, let us say, three hours. In the first few minutes he would be a hopeless addict, I think—"

"You must have known more current addicts than I have."

"Even I would not want to be pinned down. Your normal current addict is an addict after a few minutes. But then, your normal current addict asked to be made an addict, knowing what it would do to his life. Current addiction is symptomatic of despair. Your friend might have been able to fight free of a few minutes' exposure."

"So they kept him tied up for three hours. Then they cut the ropes." I felt sickened. Ordaz' ugly, ugly pictures matched mine in every detail.

"No more than three hours, by our hypothesis. They would not dare stay longer than a few hours. They would cut the ropes and leave Owen Jennison to starve to death. In the space of a month the evidence of his drugging would vanish, as would any abrasions left by ropes, lumps on his head, mercy needle punctures, and the like. A carefully detailed, well-thought-out plan, don't you agree?"

I told myself that Ordaz was not being ghoulish. He was just doing his job. Still, it was difficult to answer objectively.

"It fits our picture of Loren. He's been very careful with us. He'd love carefully detailed, well-thought-out plans."

Ordaz leaned forward. "But don't you see? A carefully detailed plan is all wrong. There is a crucial flaw in it. Suppose Mr. Jennison pulls out the droud?"

"Could he do that? Would he?"

"Could he? Certainly. A simple tug of the fingers.

The current wouldn't interfere with motor coordination. Would he?" Ordaz pulled meditatively at his beer. "I know a good deal about current addiction, but I don't know what it *feels* like, Mr. Hamilton. Your normal addict pulls his droud out as often as he inserts it, but your friend was getting ten times normal current. He might have pulled the droud out a dozen times, and instantly plugged it back each time. Yet Belters are supposed to be strong-willed men, very individualistic. Who knows whether, even after a week of addiction, your friend might not have pulled the droud loose, coiled the cord, slipped it in his pocket, and walked away scot free?

"There is the additional risk that someone might walk in on him—an automachinery serviceman, for instance. Or someone might notice that he had not bought any food in a month. A suicide would take that risk. Suicides routinely leave themselves a chance to change their minds. But a murderer?

"No. Even if the chance were one in a thousand, the man who created such a detailed plan would never have taken such a chance."

The sun burned hotly down on our shoulders. Ordaz suddenly remembered his lunch and began to eat.

I watched the world ride by beyond the hedge. Pedestrians stood in little conversational bunches; others peered into shop windows on the pedestrian strip, or glanced over the hedge to watch us eat. There were the few who pushed through the crowd with set expressions, impatient with the ten-mile-per-hour speed of the slidewalk.

"Maybe they *were* watching him. Maybe the room was bugged."

"We searched the room thoroughly," said Ordaz. "If there had been observational equipment, we would have found it."

"It could have been removed."

Ordaz shrugged.

I remembered the spy-eyes in Monica Apartments. Someone would have had to physically enter the room to carry a bug out. He could ruin it with the right signal, maybe, but it would surely leave traces.

And Owen had had an inside room. No spy-eyes.

"There's one thing you've left out," I said presently.

"And what would that be?"

"My name in Owen's wallet, listed as next of kin. He was directing my attention to the thing I was working on. The Loren gang."

"That is possible."

"You can't have it both ways."

Ordaz lowered his fork. "I *can* have it both ways, Mr. Hamilton. But you won't like it."

"I'm sure I won't."

"Let us incorporate your assumption. Mr. Jennison was contacted by an agent of Loren, the organlegger, who intended to sell transplant material to Belters. He accepted. The promise of riches was too much for him.

"A month later, something made him realize what a terrible thing he had done. He decided to die. He went to an ecstasy peddler and he had a wire put in his head. Later, before he plugged in the droud, he made one attempt to atone for his crime. He listed you as his next of kin, so that you might guess why he had died, and perhaps so that you could use that knowledge against Loren."

Ordaz looked at me across the table. "I see that you will never agree. I cannot help that. I can only read the evidence."

"Me too. But I knew Owen. He'd never have worked for an organlegger, he'd never have killed himself, and if he had, he'd never have done it that way."

Ordaz didn't answer.

"What about fingerprints?"

"In the apartment? None."

"None but Owen's?"

"Even his were found only on the chairs and end tables. I curse the man who invented the cleaning robot. Every smooth surface in that apartment was cleaned exactly forty-four times during Mr. Jennison's tenancy." Ordaz went back to his chili size.

"Then try this. Assume for the moment that I'm right. Assume Owen was after Loren, and Loren got him. Owen knew he was doing something dangerous. He wouldn't have wanted me to get onto Loren before he was ready. He wanted the reward for himself. But he might have left me something, just in case.

"Something in a locker somewhere, an airport or

spaceport locker. Evidence. Not under his own name, or mine either, because I'm a known ARM. But—"

"Some name you both know."

"Right. Like Homer Chandrasekhar. Or—got it. Cubes Forsythe. Owen would have thought that was apt. Cubes is dead."

"We will look. You must understand that it will not prove your case."

"Sure. Anything you find, Owen could have arranged in a fit of conscience. Screw that. Let me know what you get," I said, and stood up and left.

I rode the slidewalk, not caring where it was taking me. It would give me a chance to cool off.

Could Ordaz be right? Could he?

But the more I dug into Owen's death, the worse it made Owen look.

Therefore Ordaz was wrong.

Owen work for an organlegger? He'd rather have been a donor.

Owen getting his kicks from a wall socket? He never even watched tridee!

Owen kill himself? No. If so, not that way.

But even if I could have swallowed all that . . .

Owen Jennison, letting me know he'd worked with organleggers? Me, Gil the Arm Hamilton? Let *me* know *that?*

The slidewalk rolled along, past restaurants and shopping centers and churches and banks. Ten stories below, the hum of cars and scooters drifted faintly up from the vehicular level. The sky was a narrow, vivid slash of blue between black shadows of skyscraper.

Let *me* know *that?* Never.

But Ordaz' strangely inconsistent murderer was no better.

I thought of something even Ordaz had missed. Why would Loren dispose of Owen so elaborately? Owen need only disappear into the organ banks, never to bother Loren again.

The shops were thinning out now, and so were the crowds. The slidewalk narrowed, entered a residential area, and not a very good one. I'd let it carry me a long way. I looked around, trying to decide where I was.

And I was four blocks from Graham's place.

My subconscious had done me a dirty. I wanted to look at Kenneth Graham, face to face. The temptation to go on was nearly irresistible, but I fought it off and changed direction at the next disk.

A slidewalk intersection is a rotating disk, its rim tangent to four slidewalks and moving with the same speed. From the center you ride up an escalator and over the slidewalks to reach stationary walks along the buildings. I could have caught a cab at the center of the disk, but I still wanted to think, so I just rode halfway around the rim.

I could have walked into Graham's shop and gotten away with it. Maybe. I'd have looked hopeless and bored and hesitant, told Graham I wanted an ecstasy plug, worried loudly about what my wife and friends would say, then changed my mind at the last moment. He'd have let me walk out, knowing I'd be missed. Maybe.

But Loren had to know more about the ARMs than we knew about him. Some time or other, had Graham been shown a holo of yours truly? Let a known ARM walk into his shop, and Graham would panic. It wasn't worth the risk.

Then, dammit, what *could* I do?

Ordaz' inconsistent killer. If we assumed Owen was murdered, we couldn't get away from the other assumptions. The care, the nitpicking detail—and then Owen left alone to pull out the plug and walk away, or to be discovered by a persistent salesman or a burglar, or—

No. Ordaz' hypothetical killer, and mine, would have watched Owen like a hawk. For a month.

That did it. I stepped off at the next disk and got a taxi.

The taxi dropped me on the roof of Monica Apartments. I took an elevator to the lobby.

If the manager was surprised to see me, he didn't show it as he gestured me into his office. The office seemed much roomier than the lobby had, possibly because there were things to break the anonymous-modern decor: paintings on the wall, a small black worm track in the rug that must have been caused by a visitor's cigarette, a holo of Miller and his wife on the wide, nearly empty desk. He waited until I was settled, then leaned forward expectantly.

"I'm here on ARM business," I said, and passed him my ident.

He passed it back without checking it. "I presume it's the same business," he said without cordiality.

"Yah. I'm convinced Owen Jennison must have had visitors while he was here."

The manager smiled. "That's ridic—impossible."

"Nope, it's not. Your holo cameras take pictures of visitors, but they don't snap the tenants, do they?"

"Of course not."

"Then Owen could have been visited by any tenant in the building."

The manager looked shocked. "No, certainly not. Really, I don't see why you pursue this, Mr. Hamilton. If Mr. Jennison had been found in such a condition, it would have been reported!"

"I don't think so. Could he have been visited by any tenant in the building?"

"No. No. The cameras would have taken a picture of anyone from another floor."

"How about someone from the same floor?"

Reluctantly the manager bobbed his head. "Ye-es. As far as the holo cameras are concerned, that's possible. But—"

"Then I'd like to ask for pictures of any tenant who lived on the eighteenth floor during the last six weeks. Send them to the ARM Building, Central L.A. Can do?"

"Of course. You'll have them within an hour."

"Good. Now, something else occurred to me. Suppose a man got out on the nineteenth floor and walked down to the eighteenth. He'd be holoed on the nineteenth, but not on the eighteenth, right?"

The manager smiled indulgently. "Mr. Hamilton, there are no stairs in this building."

"Just the elevators? Isn't that dangerous?"

"Not at all. There is a separate self-contained emergency power source for each of the elevators. It's common practice. After all, who would want to walk up eighty stories if the elevator failed?"

"Okay, fine. One last point. Could someone tamper with the computer? Could someone make it decide not to take a certain picture, for instance?"

"I . . . am not an expert on how to tamper with computers, Mr. Hamilton. Why don't you go straight to the company? Caulfield Brains, Inc."

"Okay. What's your model?"

"Just a moment." He got up and leafed through a drawer in a filing cabinet. "EQ 144."

"Okay."

That was all I could do here, and I knew it . . . and still I didn't have the will to get up. There ought to be *something* . . .

Finally Miller cleared his throat. "Will that be all, sir?"

"Yes," I said. "No. Can I get into 1809?"

"I'll see if we've rented it yet."

"The police are through with it?"

"Certainly." He went back to the filing cabinet. "No, it's still available. I'll take you up. How long will you be?"

"I don't know. No more than half an hour. No need to come up."

"Very well." He handed me the key and waited for me to leave. I did.

The merest flicker of blue light caught my eye as I left the elevator. I would have thought it was my optic nerve, not in the real world, if I hadn't known about the holo cameras. Maybe it was. You don't need laser light to make a holograph, but it does get you clearer pictures.

Owen's room was a box. Everything was retracted. There was nothing but the bare walls. I had never seen anything so desolate, unless it was some asteroidal rock, too poor to mine, too badly placed to be worth a base.

The control panel was just beside the door. I turned on the lights, then touched the master button. Lines appeared, outlined in red and green and blue. A great square on one wall for the bed, most of another wall for the kitchen, various outlines across the floor. Very handy. You wouldn't want a guest to be standing on the table when you expanded it.

I'd come here to get the feel of the place, to encourage a hunch, to see if I'd missed anything. Translation: I was playing. Playing, I reached through the control panel to find the circuits. The printed circuitry was too small and too detailed to tell me anything, but I ran imaginary fingertips along a few wires and found that they looped straight to their action points, no detours. No sensors to the outside. You'd have to be in the room to know what was expanded, what retracted.

So a supposedly occupied room had had its bed retracted for six weeks. But you'd have to be in the room to know it.

I pushed buttons to expand the kitchen nook and the reading chair. The wall slid out eight feet; the floor humped itself and took form. I sat down in the chair, and the kitchen nook blocked my view of the door.

Nobody could have seen Owen from the hall.

If only someone had noticed that Owen wasn't ordering food. That might have saved him.

I thought of something else, and it made me look around for the air conditioner. There was a grill at floor level. I felt behind it with my imaginary hand. Some of these apartment air-conditioning units go on when the CO_2 level hits half a percent. This one was geared to temperature and manual control.

With the other kind, our careful killer could have tapped the air-conditioner current to find out if Owen was still alive and present. As it was, 1809 had behaved like an empty room for six weeks.

I flopped back in the reading chair.

If my hypothetical killer had watched Owen, he'd done it with a bug. Unless he'd actually lived on this floor for the four or five weeks it took Owen to die, there was no other way.

Okay, think about a bug. Make it small enough and nobody would find it except the cleaning robot, who would send it straight to the incinerator. You'd have to make it big, so the robot wouldn't get it. No worry about Owen finding it! And then, when you knew Owen was dead, you'd use the self-destruct.

But if you burned it to slag, you'd leave a burn hole somewhere. Ordaz would have found it. So. An asbestos pad? You'd want the self-destruct to leave something that the cleaning robot would sweep up.

And if you'll believe that you'll believe anything. It was too chancy. *Nobody* knows what a cleaning robot will decide is garbage. They're made stupid because it's cheaper. So they're programed to leave large objects alone.

There had to be someone on this floor, either to watch Owen himself or to pick up the bug that did the watching. I was betting everything I had on a human watcher.

I'd come here mainly to give my intuition a chance. It wasn't working. Owen had spent six weeks in this chair, and for at least the last week he'd been dead. Yet I couldn't feel it with him. It was just a chair with two end tables. He had left nothing in the room, not even a restless ghost.

The call caught me halfway back to Headquarters.

"You were right," Ordaz told me over the wristphone. "We have found a locker at Death Valley Port registered to Cubes Forsythe. I am on my way there now. Will you join me?"

"I'll meet you there."

"Good. I am as eager as you to see what Owen Jennison left us."

I doubted that.

The Port was something more than two hundred thirty miles away, an hour at taxi speeds. It would be a big fare. I typed out a new address on the destination board, then called in at Headquarters. An ARM agent is fairly free; he doesn't have to justify every little move. There was no question of getting permission to go. At worst they might disallow the fare on my expense account.

"Oh, and there'll be a set of holos coming in from Monica Apartments," I told the man. "Have the computer check them against known organleggers and associates of Loren."

The taxi rose smoothly into the sky and headed east. I watched tridee and drank coffee until I ran out of coins for the dispenser.

If you go between November and May, when the climate is ideal, Death Valley can be a tourist's paradise.

There is the Devil's Golf Course, with its fantastic ridges and pinnacles of salt; Zabriskie Point and its weird badlands topography; the old borax mining sites; and all kinds of strange, rare plants, adapted to the heat and the death-dry climate. Yes, Death Valley has many points of interest, and someday I was going to see them. So far all I'd seen was the spaceport. But the Port was impressive in its own way.

The landing field used to be part of a sizable inland sea. It is now a sea of salt. Alternating red and blue concentric circles mark the field for ships dropping from space, and a century's developments in chemical, fission, and fusion reaction motors have left blast pits striped like rainbows by esoteric, often radioactive salts. But mostly the field retains its ancient glare-white.

And out across the salt are ships of many sizes and many shapes. Vehicles and machinery dance attendance, and, if you're willing to wait, you may see a ship land. It's worth the wait.

The Port building, at the edge of the major salt flat, is a pastel green tower set in a wide patch of fluorescent orange concrete. No ship has ever landed on it—yet. The taxi dropped me at the entrance and moved away to join others of its kind. And I stood inhaling the dry, balmy air.

Four months of the year, Death Valley's climate is ideal. One August the Furnace Creek Ranch recorded 134° Fahrenheit shade temperature.

A man behind a desk told me that Ordaz had arrived before me. I found him and another officer in a labyrinth of pay lockers, each big enough to hold two or three suitcases. The locker Ordaz had opened held only a lightweight plastic briefcase.

"He may have taken other lockers," he said.

"Probably not. Belters travel light. Have you tried to open it?"

"Not yet. It is a combination lock. I thought perhaps . . ."

"Maybe." I squatted to look at it.

Funny: I felt no surprise at all. It was as if I'd known all along that Owen's suitcase would be there. And why not? He was bound to try to protect himself somehow. Through me, because I was already involved in the UN side of organlegging. By leaving something in a space-port locker, because Loren couldn't find the right locker or get into it if he did, and because I would naturally connect Owen with spaceports. Under Cubes' name, be-cause I'd be looking for that, and Loren wouldn't.

Hindsight is wonderful.

The lock had five digits. "He must have meant me to open it. Let's see . . ." and I moved the tumblers to 42217. April 22, 2117, the day Cubes died, stapled sud-denly to a plastic partition.

The lock clicked open.

Ordaz went instantly for the manila folder. More slowly, I picked up two glass phials. One was tightly sealed against Earth's air, and half full of an incredibly fine dust. So fine was it that it slid about like oil inside the glass. The other phial held a blackened grain of nickel-iron, barely big enough to see.

Other things were in that case, but the prize was that folder. The story was in there . . . at least up to a point. Owen must have planned to add to it.

A message had been waiting for him in the Ceres mail dump when he returned from his last trip out. Owen must have laughed over parts of that message. Loren had taken the trouble to assemble a complete dossier of Owen's smuggling activities over the past eight years. Did he think he could ensure Owen's silence by threat-ening to turn the dossier over to the goldskins?

Maybe the dossier had given Owen the wrong idea. In any case, he'd decided to contact Loren and see what developed. Ordinarily he'd have sent me the entire mes-sage and let me try to track it down. I was the expert, after all. But Owen's last trip out had been a disaster.

His fusion drive had blown somewhere beyond Jupi-ter's orbit. No explanation. The safeties had blown his lifesystem capsule free of the explosion, barely. A rescue ship had returned him to Ceres. The fee had nearly bro-ken him. He needed money. Loren may have known that, and counted on it.

The reward for information leading to Loren's cap-ture would have bought him a new ship.

He'd landed at Outback Field, following Loren's in-structions. From there, Loren's men had moved him about a good deal: to London, to Bombay, to Amberg, Germany. Owen's personal, written story ended in Amberg. How had he reached California? He had not had a chance to say.

But in between, he had learned a good deal. There were snatches of detail on Loren's organization. There was Loren's full plan for shipping illicit transplant materials to the Belt, and for finding and contacting customers. Owen had made suggestions there. Most of them sounded reasonable and would be unworkable in practice. Typically Owen. I could find no sign that he'd overplayed his hand.

But of course he hadn't known it when he did.

And there were holos, twenty-three of them, each a member of Loren's gang. Some of the pictures had markings on the back; others were blank. Owen had been unable to find out where each of them stood in the organization.

I leafed through them twice, wondering if one of them could be Loren himself. Owen had never known.

"It would seem you were right," said Ordáz. "He could not have collected such detail by accident. He must have planned from the beginning to betray the Loren gang."

"Just as I told you. And he was murdered for it."

"It seems he must have been. What motive could he have had for suicide?" Ordaz' round, calm face was doing its best to show anger. "I find I cannot believe in our inconsistent murderer either. You have ruined my digestion, Mr. Hamilton."

I told him my idea about other tenants on Owen's floor. He nodded. "Possibly, possibly. This is your department now. Organlegging is the business of the ARMs."

"Right." I closed the briefcase and hefted it. "Let's see what the computer can do with these. I'll send you photocopies of everything in here."

"You'll let me know about the other tenants?"

"Of course."

I walked into ARM Headquarters swinging that precious briefcase, feeling on top of the world. Owen had been murdered. He had died with honor, if not—oh, definitely not—with dignity. Even Ordaz knew it now.

Then Jackson Bera, snarling and panting, went by at a dead run.

"What's up?" I called after him. Maybe I wanted a chance to brag. I had twenty-three faces, twenty-three organleggers, in my briefcase.

Bera slid to a stop beside me. "Where *you* been?"

"Working. Honest. What's the hurry?"

"Remember that pleasure peddler we were watching?"

"Graham? Kenneth Graham?"

"That's the one. He's dead. We blew it." And Bera took off.

He'd reached the lab by the time I caught up with him.

Kenneth Graham's corpse was face up on the operating table. His long, lantern-jawed face was pale and slack, without expression; empty. Machinery was in place above and below his head.

"How you doing?" Bera demanded.

"Not good," the doctor answered. "Not your fault. You got him into the deepfreeze fast enough. It's just that the current—" he shrugged.

I shook Bera's shoulder. "What happened?"

Bera was panting a little from his run. "Something must have leaked. Graham tried to make a run for it. We got him at the airport."

"You could have waited. Put someone on the plane with him. Flooded the plane with TY-4."

"Remember the stink the last time we used TY-4 on civilians? Damn newscasters." Bera was shivering. I didn't blame him.

ARMs and organleggers play a funny kind of game. The organleggers have to turn their donors in alive, so they're always armed with hypo guns, firing slivers of crystalline anesthetic that melt instantly in the blood. We use the same weapon, for somewhat the same reason: a ʳiminal has to be saved for trial, and then for the govᵐent hospitals. So no ARM ever expects to kill a

ʳe was a day I learned the truth. A small-time organlegger named Raphael Haine was trying to reach a call button in his own home. If he'd reached it all kinds of hell would have broken loose, Haine's men would have hypoed me, and I would have regained consciousness a piece at a time, in Haine's organ-storage tanks. So I strangled him.

The report was in the computer, but only three human beings knew about it. One was my immediate superior, Lucas Carner. The other was Julie. So far, he was the only man I'd ever killed.

And Graham was Bera's first killing.

"We got him at the airport," said Bera. "He was wearing a hat. I wish I'd noticed that, we might have moved faster. We started to close in on him with hypo guns. He turned and saw us. He reached under his hat, and then he fell."

"Killed himself?"

"Uh huh."

"How?"

"Look at his head."

I edged closer to the table, trying to stay out of the doctor's way. The doctor was going through the routine of trying to pull information from a dead brain by induction. It wasn't going well.

There was a flat oblong box on top of Graham's head. Black plastic, about half the size of a pack of cards. I touched it and knew at once that it was attached to Graham's skull.

"A droud. Not a standard type. Too big."

"Uh huh."

Liquid helium ran up my nerves. "There's a battery in it."

"Right."

"I often wonder what the vintners buy, et cetera. A cordless droud. Man, that's what *I* want for Christmas."

Bera twitched all over. "Don't *say* that."

"Did you know he was a current addict?"

"No. We were afraid to bug his home. He might have found it and been tipped. Take another look at that thing."

The shape was wrong, I thought. The black plastic case had been half melted.

"Heat," I mused. "Oh!"

"Uh huh. He blew the whole battery at once. Sent the whole killing charge right through his brain, right through the pleasure center of his brain. And, Jesus, Gil, the thing I keep wondering is, what did it feel like? Gil, what could it possibly have *felt* like?"

I thumped him across the shoulders in lieu of giving him an intelligent answer. He'd be a long time wondering. And so would I.

Here was the man who had put the wire in Owen's head. Had his death been momentary Hell, or all the delights of paradise in one singing jolt? Hell, I hoped, but I didn't believe it.

At least Kenneth Graham wasn't somewhere else in the world, getting a new face and new retinas and new fingertips from Loren's illicit organ banks.

"Nothing," said the doctor. "His brain's too badly burned. There's just nothing there that isn't too scrambled to make sense."

"Keep trying," said Bera.

I left quietly. Maybe later I'd buy Bera a drink. He seemed to need it. Bera was one of those with empathy. I knew that he could almost feel that awful surge of ecstasy and defeat as Kenneth Graham left the world behind.

The holos from Monica Apartments had arrived hours ago. Miller had picked not only the tenants who had occupied the eighteenth floor during the past six weeks, but tenants from the nineteenth and seventeenth floors too. It seemed an embarrassment of riches. I toyed with the idea of someone from the nineteenth floor dropping over his balcony to the eighteenth, every day for five weeks. But 1809 hadn't had an outside wall, let alone a window, not to mention a balcony.

Had Miller played with the same idea? Nonsense. He didn't even know the problem. He'd just overkilled with the holos to show how cooperative he was.

None of the tenants during the period in question matched known or suspected Loren men.

I said a few appropriate words and went for coffee. Then I remembered the twenty-three possible Loren in Owen's briefcase. I'd left them with a programer, since I wasn't quite sure how to get them into the computer myself. He ought to be finished by now.

I called down. He was.

I persuaded the computer to compare them with the holos from Monica Apartments.

Nothing. Nobody matched anybody.

I spent the next two hours writing up the Owen Jennison case. A programer would have to translate it for the machine. I wasn't that good yet.

We were back with Ordaz' inconsistent killer.

That, and a tangle of dead ends. Owen's death had bought us a handful of new pictures, pictures which might even be obsolete by now. Organleggers changed their faces at the drop of a hat. I finished the case outline, sent it down to a programer, and called Julie. I wouldn't need her protection now.

Julie had left for home.

I started to call Taffy, stopped with her number half dialed. There are times not to make a phone call. I needed to sulk; I needed a cave to be alone in. My expression would probably have broken a phone screen. Why inflict it on an innocent girl?

I left for home.

It was dark when I reached the street. I rode the pedestrian bridge across the slidewalks, waited for a taxi at the intersection disk. Presently one dropped, the white FREE sign blinking on its belly. I stepped in and deposited my credit card.

Owen had collected his holos from all over the Eurasian continent. Most of them, if not all, had been Loren's foreign agents. Why had I expected to find them in Los Angeles?

The taxi rose into the white night sky. City lights turned the cloud cover into a flat white dome. We penetrated the clouds, and stayed there. The taxi autopilot didn't care if I had a view or not.

. . . So what did I have now? Someone among dozens of tenants was a Loren man. That, or Ordaz' inconsistent killer, the careful one, had left Owen to die for five weeks, alone and unsupervised.

. . . Was the inconsistent killer so unbelievable?

He was, after all, my own hypothetical Loren. And Loren had committed murder, the ultimate crime. He'd murdered routinely, over and over, with fabulous profits. The ARMs hadn't been able to touch him. Wasn't it about time he started getting careless?

Like Graham. How long had Graham been selecting donors among his customers, choosing a few nonentities a year? And then, twice within a few months, he took clients who were missed. Careless.

Most criminals are not too bright. Loren had brains enough; but the men on his payroll would be about average. Loren would deal with the stupid ones, the ones who turned to crime because they didn't have enough sense to make it in real life.

If a man like Loren got careless, this was how it would happen. Unconsciously he would judge ARM intelligence by his own men. Seduced by an ingenious plan for murder, he might ignore the single loophole and go through with it. With Graham to advise him, he knew more about current addiction than we did; perhaps enough to trust the effects of current addiction on Owen.

Then Owen's killers had delivered him to his apartment and never seen him again. It was a small gamble Loren had taken, and it had paid off, this time.

Next time he'd grow more careless. One day we'd get him.

But not today.

The taxi settled out of the traffic pattern, touched down on the roof of my apartment building in the Hollywood Hills. I got out and moved toward the elevators.

An elevator opened. Someone stepped out.

Something warned me, something about the way he moved. I turned, quick-drawing from the shoulder. The taxi might have made good cover—if it hadn't been already rising. Other figures had stepped from the shadows.

I think I got a couple before something stung my cheek. Mercy-bullets, slivers of crystalline anesthetic melting in my bloodstream. My head spun, and the roof spun, and the centrifugal force dropped me limply to the roof. Shadows loomed above me, then receded to infinity.

Fingers on my scalp shocked me awake.

I woke standing upright, bound like a mummy in soft, swaddling bandages. I couldn't so much as twitch a muscle below my neck. By the time I knew that much it was too late. The man behind me had finished removing electrodes from my head and stepped into view, out of reach of my imaginary arm.

There was something of the bird about him. He was tall and slender, small-boned, and his triangular face reached a point at the chin. His wild, silken blond hair had withdrawn from his temples, leaving a sharp widow's peak. He wore impeccably tailored wool street shorts in orange and brown stripes. Smiling brightly, with his arms folded and his head cocked to one side, he stood waiting for me to speak.

And I recognized him. Owen had taken a holo of him, somewhere.

"Where am I?" I groaned, trying to sound groggy. "What time is it?"

"Time? It's already morning," said my captor. "As for where you are, I'll let you wonder."

Something about his manner . . . I took a guess and said, "Loren?"

Loren bowed, not overdoing it. "And you are Gilbert Hamilton of the United Nations Police. Gil the Arm."

Had he said Arm or ARM? I let it pass. "I seem to have slipped."

"You underestimated the reach of my own arm. You also underestimated my interest."

I had. It isn't much harder to capture an ARM than any other citizen, if you catch him off guard, and if you're willing to risk the men. In this case his risk had cost him nothing. Cops use hypo guns for the same reason organleggers do. The men I'd shot, if I'd hit anyone in those few seconds of battle, would have come around long ago. Loren must have set me up in these bandages, then left me under "russian sleep" until he was ready to talk to me.

The electrodes were the "russian sleep." One goes on each eyelid, one on the nape of the neck. A small cur-

rent goes through the brain, putting you right to sleep.
You get a full night's sleep in an hour. If it's not turned
off you can sleep forever.

So this was Loren.

He stood watching me with his head cocked to one
side, birdlike, with his arms folded. One hand held a
hypo gun, rather negligently, I thought.

What time was it? I didn't dare ask again, because
Loren might guess something. But if I could stall him
until 0945, Julie could send help . . .

She could send help where?

Finagle in hysterics! Where was I? If I didn't know
that, Julie wouldn't know either!

And Loren intended me for the organ banks. One
crystalline sliver would knock me out without harming
any of the delicate, infinitely various parts that made me
Gil Hamilton. Then Loren's doctors would take me
apart.

In government operating rooms they flash-burn the
criminal's brain for later urn burial. God knows what
Loren would do with my own brain. But the rest of me
was young and healthy. Even considering Loren's overhead, I was worth more than a million UN marks on the
hoof.

"Why me?" I asked. "It was me you wanted, not just
any ARM. Why the interest in me?"

"It was you who were investigating the case of Owen
Jennison. *Much* too thoroughly."

"Not thoroughly enough, dammit!"

Loren looked puzzled. "You really don't understand?"

"I really don't."

"I find that highly interesting," Loren mused. "Highly."

"All right, why am I still alive?"

"I was curious, Mr. Hamilton. I hoped you'd tell me
about your imaginary arm."

So he'd said Arm, not ARM. I bluffed anyway. "My
what?"

"No need for games, Mr. Hamilton. If I think I'm
losing I'll use this." He wiggled the hypo gun. "You'll
never wake up."

Damn! He knew. The only things I could move were

my ears and my imaginary arm, and Loren knew all
about it! I'd never be able to lure him into reach.

Provided he knew *all* about it.

I had to draw him out.

"Okay," I said, "but I'd like to know how you found
out about it. A plant in the ARMs?"

Loren chuckled. "I wish it were so. No. We captured
one of your men some months ago, quite by accident.
When I realized what he was, I induced him to talk shop
with me. He was able to tell me something about your
remarkable arm. I hope you'll tell me more."

"Who was it?"

"Really, Mr. Hamil—"

"Who was it?"

"Do you really expect me to remember the name of
every donor?"

Who had gone into Loren's organ banks? Stranger,
acquaintance, friend? Does the manager of a slaughter-
house remember every slaughtered steer?

"So-called psychic powers interest me," said Loren.
"I remembered you. And then, when I was on the verge
of concluding an agreement with your Belter friend Jennison, I remembered something unusual about a crewman he had shipped with. They called you Gil the Arm,
didn't they? Prophetic. In port your drinks came free if
you could use your imaginary arm to drink them."

"Then damn you. You thought Owen was a plant, did
you? Because of me! Me!"

"Breast beating will earn you nothing, Mr. Hamilton." Loren put steel in his voice. "Entertain me, Mr.
Hamilton."

I'd been feeling around for anything that might release me from my upright prison. No such luck. I was
wrapped like a mummy in bandages too strong to break.
All I could feel with my imaginary hand were cloth
bandages up to my neck, and a bracing rod along my
back to hold me upright. Beneath the swathing I was naked.

"I'll show you my eldritch powers," I told Loren, "if
you'll loan me a cigarette." Maybe that would draw him
close enough . . .

He knew something about my arm. He knew its
reach. He put one single cigarette on the edge of a small

table-on-wheels and slid it up to me. I picked it up and stuck it in my mouth and waited hopefully for him to come light it. "My mistake," he murmured; and he pulled the table back and repeated the whole thing with a lighted cigarette.

No luck. At least I'd gotten my smoke. I pitched the dead one as far as it would go: about two feet. I have to move slowly with my imaginary hand. Otherwise what I'm holding simply slips through my fingers.

Loren watched in fascination. A floating, disembodied cigarette, obeying my will! His eyes held traces of awe and horror. That was bad. Maybe the cigarette had been a mistake.

Some people see psi powers as akin to witchcraft, and psychic people as servants of Satan. If Loren feared me, then I was dead.

"Interesting," said Loren. "How far will it reach?"

He knew that. "As far as my real arm, of course."

"But why? Others can reach much further. Why not you?"

He was clear across the room, a good ten yards away, sprawled in an armchair. One hand held a drink, the other held the hypo gun. He was superbly relaxed. I wondered if I'd ever see him move from that comfortable chair, much less come within reach.

The room was small and bare, with the look of a basement. Loren's chair and a small portable bar were the only furnishings, unless there were others behind me.

A basement could be anywhere. Anywhere in Los Angeles, or out of it. If it was really morning, I could be anywhere on Earth by now.

"Sure," I said, "others can reach further than me. But they don't have my strength. It's an imaginary arm, sure enough, and my imagination won't make it ten feet long. Maybe someone could convince me it was, if he tried hard enough. But maybe he'd ruin what belief I have. Then I'd have two arms, just like everyone else. I'm better off . . ." I let it trail away, because Loren was going to take all my damn arms anyway.

My cigarette was finished. I pitched it away.

"Want a drink?"

"Sure, if you've got a jigger glass. Otherwise I can't lift it."

He found me a shot glass and sent it to me on the edge of the rolling table. I was barely strong enough to pick it up. Loren's eyes never left me as I sipped and put it down.

The old cigarette lure. Last night I'd used it to pick up a girl. Now it was keeping me alive.

Did I really want to leave the world with something gripped tightly in my imaginary fists? Entertaining Loren. Holding his interest until—

Where was I? Where?

And suddenly I knew. "We're at Monica Apartments," I said. "Nowhere else."

"I knew you'd guess that eventually." Loren smiled. "But it's too late. I got to you in time."

"Don't be so damn complacent. It was my stupidity, not your luck. I should have *smelled* it. Owen would never have come here of his own choice. You ordered him here."

"And so I did. By then I already knew he was a traitor."

"So you sent him here to die. Who was it that checked on him every day to see he'd stayed put? Was it Miller, the manager? He has to be working for you. He's the one who took the holographs of you and your men out of the computer."

"He was the one," said Loren. "But it wasn't every day. I had a man watching Jennison every second, through a portable camera. We took it out after he was dead."

"And then waited a week. Nice touch." The wonder was that it had taken me so long. The atmosphere of the place . . . what kind of people would live in Monica Apartments? The faceless ones, the ones with no identity, the ones who would surely be missed by nobody. They would stay put in their apartments while Loren checked on them, to see that they really did have nobody to miss them. Those who qualified would disappear, and their papers and possessions with them, and their holos would vanish from the computer.

Loren said, "I tried to sell organs to the Belters,

through your friend Jennison. I know he betrayed me, Hamilton. I want to know how badly."

"Badly enough." He'd guess that. "We've got detailed plans for setting up an organ-bank dispensary in the Belt. It wouldn't have worked anyway, Loren. Belters don't think that way."

"No pictures."

"No." I didn't want him changing his face.

"I was sure he'd left something," said Loren. "Otherwise we'd have made him a donor. Much simpler. More profitable, too. I needed the money, Hamilton. Do you know what it costs the organization to let a donor go?"

"A million or so. Why'd you do it?"

"He'd left something. There was no way to get at it. All we could do was try to keep the ARMs from looking for it."

"Ah." I had it then. "When anyone disappears without a trace, the first thing any idiot thinks of is organleggers."

"Naturally. So he couldn't just disappear, could he? The police would go to the ARMs, the file would go to you, and you'd start looking."

"For a spaceport locker."

"Oh?"

"Under the name of Cubes Forsythe."

"I knew that name," Loren said between his teeth. "I should have tried that. You know, after we had him hooked on current, we tried pulling the plug on him to get him to talk. It didn't work. He couldn't concentrate on anything but getting the droud back in his head. We looked high and low—"

"I'm going to kill you," I said, and meant every word.

Loren cocked his head, frowning. "On the contrary, Mr. Hamilton. Another cigarette?"

"Yah."

He sent it to me, lighted, on the rolling table. I picked it up, holding it a trifle ostentatiously. Maybe I could focus his attention on it—on his only way to find my imaginary hand.

Because if he kept his eyes on the cigarette, and I put it in my mouth at a crucial moment—I'd leave my hand free without his noticing.

What crucial moment? He was still in the armchair. I had to fight the urge to coax him closer. Any move in that direction would make him suspicious.

What time was it? And what was Julie doing? I thought of a night two weeks past. Remembered dinner on the balcony of the highest restaurant in Los Angeles, just a fraction less than a mile up. A carpet of neon that spread below us to touch the horizon in all directions. Maybe she'd pick it up . . .

She'd be checking on me at 0945.

"You must have made a remarkable spaceman," said Loren. "Think of being the only man in the solar system who can adjust a hull antenna without leaving the cabin."

"Antennas take a little more muscle than I've got." So he knew I could reach through things. If he'd seen that far—"I should have stayed," I told Loren. "I wish I were on a mining ship, right this minute. All I wanted at the time was two good arms."

"Pity. Now you have three. Did it occur to you that using psi powers against men was a form of cheating?"

"What?"

"Remember Raphael Haine?" Loren's voice had become uneven. He was angry, and holding it down with difficulty.

"Sure. Small-time organlegger in Australia."

"Raphael Haine was a friend of mine. I know he had you tied up at one point. Tell me, Mr. Hamilton: if your imaginary hand is as weak as you say, how did you untie the ropes?"

"I didn't. I couldn't have. Haine used handcuffs. I picked his pocket for the key . . . with my imaginary hand, of course."

"You used psi powers against him. You had no right!"

Magic. Anyone who's not psychic himself feels the same way, just a little. A touch of dread, a touch of envy. Loren thought he could handle ARMs; he'd killed at least one of us. But to send warlocks against him was grossly unfair.

That was why he'd let me wake up. Loren wanted to gloat. How many men have captured a warlock?

"Don't be an idiot," I said. "I didn't volunteer to play your silly game, or Haine's either. *My* rules make you a wholesale murderer."

Loren got to his feet (what time was it?) and I suddenly realized my time was up. He was in a white rage. His silky blond hair seemed to stand on end.

I looked into the tiny needle hole in the hypo gun. There was nothing I could do. The reach of my TK was the reach of my fingers. I felt all the things I would never feel: the quart of Trastine in my blood to keep the water from freezing in my cells, the cold bath of half-frozen alcohol, the scalpels and the tiny, accurate surgical lasers. Most of all, the scalpels.

And my knowledge would die when they threw away my brain. I knew what Loren looked like. I knew about Monica Apartments, and who knew how many others of the same kind? I knew where to go to find all the loveliness in Death Valley, and someday I was going to go. What time was it? What time?

Loren had raised the hypo gun and was sighting down the stiff length of his arm. Obviously he thought he was at target practice. "It really is a pity," he said, and there was only the slightest tremor in his voice. "You should have stayed a spaceman."

What was he waiting for? "I can't cringe unless you loosen these bandages," I snapped, and I jabbed what was left of my cigarette at him for emphasis. It jerked out of my grip, and I reached and caught it and—

And stuck it in my left eye.

At another time I'd have examined the idea a little more closely. But I'd still have done it. Loren already thought of me as his property. As live skin and healthy kidneys and lengths of artery, as parts in Loren's organ banks, I was property worth a million UN marks. And I was destroying my eye! Organleggers are always hurting for eyes; anyone who wears glasses could use a new pair, and the organleggers themselves are constantly wanting to change retina prints.

What I hadn't anticipated was the pain. I'd read somewhere that there are no sensory nerves in the eyeball. Then it was my lids that hurt. Terribly!

But I only had to hold on for a moment.

Loren swore and came for me at a dead run. He

knew how terribly weak was my imaginary arm. What could I do with it? He didn't know; he'd never known, though it stared him in the face. He ran at me and slapped at the cigarette, a full swing that half knocked my head off my neck and sent the now dead butt ricocheting off a wall. Panting, snarling, speechless with rage, he stood—within reach.

My eye closed like a small tormented fist.

I reached past Loren's gun, through his chest wall, and found his heart. And squeezed.

His eyes became very round, his mouth gaped wide, his larynx bobbed convulsively. There was time to fire the gun. Instead he clawed at his chest with a half-paralyzed arm. Twice he raked his fingernails across his chest, gaping upward for air that wouldn't come. He thought he was having a heart attack. Then his rolling eyes found my face.

My face. I was a one-eyed carnivore, snarling with the will to murder. I would have his life if I had to tear the heart out of his chest! How could he help but know?

He knew!

He fired at the floor, and fell.

I was sweating and shaking with reaction and disgust. The scars! He was all scars; I'd felt them going in. His heart was a transplant. And the rest of him—he'd looked about thirty from a distance, but this close it was impossible to tell. Parts were younger, parts older. How much of Loren was Loren? What parts had he taken from others? And none of the parts quite matched.

He must have been chronically ill, I thought. And the Board wouldn't give him the transplants he needed. And one day he'd seen the answer to all his problems . . .

Loren wasn't moving. He wasn't breathing. I remembered the way his heart had jumped and wriggled in my imaginary hand, and then suddenly given up.

He was lying on his left arm, hiding his watch. I was all alone in an empty room, and I still didn't know what time it was.

I never found out. It was hours before Miller finally dared to interrupt his boss. He stuck his round, blank face around the door jamb, saw Loren sprawled at my feet, and darted back with a squeak. A minute later a hypo gun came around the jamb, followed by a watery blue eye. I felt the sting in my cheek.

"I checked you early," said Julie. She settled herself uncomfortably at the foot of the hospital bed. "Rather, you called me. When I came to work you weren't there, and I wondered why, and *wham*. It was bad, wasn't it?"

"Pretty bad," I said.

"I've never sensed anyone so scared."

"Well, don't tell anyone about it." I hit the switch to raise the bed to sitting position. "I've got an image to maintain."

My eye and the socket around it were bandaged and numb. There was no pain, but the numbness was obtrusive, a reminder of two dead men who had become part of me. One arm, one eye.

If Julie was feeling that with me, then small wonder if she was nervous. She was. She kept shifting and twisting on the bed.

"I kept wondering what time it was. What time was it?"

"About nine-ten." Julie shivered. "I thought I'd faint when that—that vague little man pointed his hypo gun around the corner. Oh, don't! Don't, Gil. It's *over*."

That close? Was it *that* close? "Look," I said, "you go back to work. I appreciate the sick call, but this isn't doing either of us any good. If we keep it up we'll both wind up in a state of permanent terror."

She nodded jerkily and got up.

"Thanks for coming. Thanks for saving my life too."

Julie smiled from the doorway. "Thanks for the orchids."

I hadn't ordered them yet. I flagged down a nurse and got her to tell me that I could leave tonight, after dinner, provided I went straight home to bed. She brought me a phone, and I used it to order the orchids.

Afterward I dropped the bed back and lay there awhile. It was nice being alive. I began to remember promises I had made, promises I might never have kept. Perhaps it was time to keep a few.

I called down to Surveillance and got Jackson Bera. After letting him drag from me the story of my heroism, I invited him up to the infirmary for a drink. His bottle, but I'd pay. He didn't like that part, but I bullied him into it.

I had dialed half of Taffy's number before, as I had last night, I changed my mind. My wristphone was on the bedside table. No pictures.

" 'Lo."

"Taffy? This is Gil. Can you get a weekend free?"

"Sure. Starting Friday?"

"Good."

"Come for me at ten. Did you ever find out about your friend?"

"Yah. I was right. Organleggers killed him. It's over now, we got the guy in charge." I didn't mention the eye. By Friday the bandages would be off. "About that weekend. How would you like to see Death Valley?"

"You're kidding, right?"

"I'm kidding, wrong. Listen—"

"But it's hot! It's dry! It's as dead as the Moon! You did say Death Valley, didn't you?"

"It's not hot this month. Listen . . ." And she did listen. She listened long enough to be convinced.

"I've been thinking," she said then. "If we're going to see a lot of each other, we'd better make a—a bargain. No shop talk. All right?"

"A good idea."

"The point is, I work in a hospital," said Taffy. "Surgery. To me, organic transplant material is just the tools of my trade, tools to use in healing. It took me a long time to get that way. I don't want to know where the stuff comes from, and I don't want to know anything about organleggers."

"Okay, we've got a covenant. See you at ten hundred Friday."

A doctor, I thought afterward. Well. The weekend was going to be a good one. Surprising people are always the ones most worth knowing.

Bera came in with a pint of J&B. "My treat," he said. "No use arguing, 'cause you can't reach your wallet anyway." And the fight was on.

THE DEFENSELESS DEAD

The dead lay side by side beneath the glass. Long ago, in a roomier world, these older ones had been entombed each in his own double-walled casket. Now they lay shoulder to shoulder, more or less in chronological order, looking up, their features clear through thirty centimeters of liquid nitrogen sandwiched between two thick sheets of glass.

Elsewhere in the building some sleepers wore clothing, formal costumery of a dozen periods. In two long tanks on another floor the sleepers had been prettied up with low-temperature cosmetics, and sometimes with a kind of flesh-colored putty to fill and cover major wounds. A weird practice. It hadn't lasted beyond the middle of the last century. After all, these sleepers planned to return to life someday. The damage should show at a glance.

With these, it did.

They were all from the tail end of the twentieth century. They looked like hell. Some were clearly beyond saving, accident cases whose wills had consigned them to the freezer banks regardless. Each sleeper was marked by a plaque describing everything that was wrong with his mind and body, in script so fine and so archaic as to be almost unreadable.

Battered or torn or wasted by disease, they all wore the same look of patient resignation. Their hair was disintegrating, very slowly. It had fallen in a thick gray crescent about each head.

"People used to call them *corpsicles,* frozen dead. Or *Homo snapiens.* You can imagine what would happen if you dropped one." Mr. Restarick did not smile. These people were in his charge, and he took his task serious-ly. His eyes seemed to look through rather than at me, and his clothes were ten to fifty years out of style. He seemed to be gradually losing himself here in the past. He said, "We've over six thousand of them here. Do you think we'll ever bring them back to life?" I was an ARM, I might know.

"Do you?"

"Sometimes I wonder." He dropped his gaze. "Not Harrison Cohn. Look at him, torn open like that. And *her,* with half her face shot off; she'd be a vegetable if you brought her back. The later ones don't look this bad. Up until 1989 the doctors couldn't freeze anyone who wasn't clinically dead."

"That doesn't make *sense.* Why not?"

"They'd have been up for murder. When what they were doing was *saving* lives." He shrugged angrily. "Sometimes they'd stop a patient's heart and then restart it, to satisfy the legalities."

Sure, that made a lot of sense. I didn't dare laugh out loud. I pointed. "How about him?"

He was a rangy man of about forty-five, healthy-look-ing, with no visible marks of death, violent or otherwise. The long lean face still wore a look of command, though the deep-set eyes were almost closed. His lips were slightly parted, showing teeth straightened by braces in the ancient fashion.

Mr. Restarick glanced at the plaque. "Leviticus Hale, 1991. Oh, yes. Hale was a paranoid. He must have been the first they ever froze for *that.* They guessed right, too. If we brought him back now we could cure him."

"If."

"It's been done."

"Sure. We only lose one out of three. He'd probably take the chance himself. But then, he's crazy." I looked around at rows of long double-walled liquid nitrogen tanks. The place was huge and full of echoes, and this was only the top floor. The Vault of Eternity was ten stories deep in earthquake-free bedrock. "Six thousand, you said. But the Vault was built for ten thousand, wasn't it?"

He nodded. "We're a third empty."

"Get many customers these days?"

He laughed at me. "You're joking. Nobody has himself frozen these days. He might wake up a piece at a time!"

"That's what I wondered."

"Ten years ago we were thinking of digging new vaults. All those crazy kids, perfectly healthy, getting themselves frozen so they could wake up in a brave new world. I had to watch while the ambulances came and carted them away for spare parts! We're a good third empty now since the Freezer Law passed!"

That business with the kids had been odd, all right. A fad or a religion or a madness, except that it had gone on for much too long.

The Freezeout Kids. Most of them were textbook cases of *anomie,* kids in their late teens who felt trapped in an imperfect world. History taught them (those that listened) that earlier times had been much worse. Perhaps they thought that the world was moving toward perfection.

Some had gambled. Not many in any given year; but it had been going on ever since the first experimental freezer vault revivals, a generation before I was born. It was better than suicide. They were young, they were healthy, they stood a better chance of revival than any of the frozen, damaged dead. They were poorly adapted to their society. Why not risk it?

Two years ago they had been answered. The General Assembly and the world vote had passed the Freezer Bill into law.

There were those in frozen sleep who had not had the foresight to set up a trust fund, or who had selected the wrong trustee or invested in the wrong stocks. If medicine or a miracle had revived them now, they would have been on the dole, with no money and no trace of useful education and, in about half the cases, no evident ability to survive in *any* society.

Were they in frozen sleep or frozen death? In law there had always been that point of indecision. The Freezer Law cleared it up to some extent. It declared any person in frozen sleep, who could not support himself should society choose to reawaken him, to be dead in law.

And a third of the world's frozen dead, twelve

hundred thousand of them, had gone into the organ banks.

"You were in charge then?"

The old man nodded. "I've been on the day shift at the Vault for almost forty years. I watched the ambulances fly away with three thousand of my people. I think of them as my people," he said a bit defensively.

"The law can't seem to decide if they're alive or dead. Think of them any way you like."

"People who trusted me. What did those Freezeout Kids do that was worth killing them for?"

I thought: they wanted to sleep it out while others broke their backs turning the world into Paradise. But it's no capital crime.

"They had nobody to defend them. Nobody but me." He trailed off. After a bit, and with visible effort, he pulled himself back to the present. "Well, never mind. What can I do for the United Nations police, Mr. Hamilton?"

"Oh, I'm not here as an ARM agent. I'm just here to, to—" Hell, I didn't know myself. It was a news broadcast that had jarred me into coming here. I said, "They're planning to introduce another Freezer Bill."

"What?"

"A second Freezer Bill. Naming a different group. The communal organ banks must be empty again," I said bitterly.

Mr. Restarick started to shake. "Oh, no. No. They can't do that again. They, they can't."

I gripped his arm, to reassure him or to hold him up. He looked about to faint. "Maybe they can't. The first Freezer Law was supposed to stop organlegging, but it didn't. Maybe the citizens will vote this one down."

I left as soon as I could.

The second Freezer Bill made slow, steady progress, without much opposition. I caught some of it in the boob cube. A perturbingly large number of citizens were petitioning the Security Council for confiscation of what they described as "The frozen corpses of a large number of people who were insane when they died. Parts of these corpses could possibly be recovered for badly needed organ replacements . . ."

They never mentioned that said corpses might someday be recovered whole and living. They often mentioned that said corpses could not be safely recovered
now; and they could prove it with experts; and they had
a thousand experts waiting their turns to testify.

They never mentioned biochemical cures for insanity.
They spoke of the lack of a world-wide need for mental
patients and for insanity-carrying genes.

They hammered constantly on the need for organ
transplant material.

I just about gave up watching news broadcasts. I was
an ARM, a member of the United Nations police force,
and I wasn't supposed to get involved in politics. It was
none of my business.

It didn't become my business until I ran across a familiar name, eleven months later.

Taffy was peoplewatching. That demure look didn't
fool me. A secretive glee looked out of her soft brown
eyes, and they shifted left every time she raised her dessert spoon.

I didn't try to follow her eyes for fear of blowing her
cover. Come, I will conceal nothing from you: I don't
care who's eating at the next table in a public restaurant.
Instead I lit a cigarette, shifted it to my imaginary hand
(the weight tugging gently at my mind) and settled back
to enjoy my surroundings.

High Cliffs is an enormous pyramidal city-in-a-build-
ing in northern California. Midgard is on the first shopping level, way back near the service core. There's no
view, but the restaurant makes up for it with a spectacu-
lar set of environment walls.

From inside, Midgard seems to be halfway up the
trunk of an enormous tree, big enough to stretch from
Hell to Heaven. Perpetual war is waged in the vasty dis-
tances, on various limbs of the tree, between warriors of
oddly distorted size and shape. World-sized beasts show
occasionally: a wolf attacks the moon, a sleeping serpent coils round the restaurant itself, the eye of a curious brown squirrel suddenly blocks one row of windows . . .

"Isn't that Holden Chambers?"

"Who?" The name sounded vaguely familiar.

"Four tables over, sitting alone."

I looked. He was tall and skinny, and much younger than most of Midgard's clientele. Long blond hair, weak chin—he was really the type who ought to grow a beard. I was sure I'd never seen him before.

Taffy frowned. "I wonder why he's eating alone. Do you suppose someone broke a date?"

The name clicked. "Holden Chambers. Kidnapping case. Someone kidnapped him and his sister, years ago. One of Bera's cases."

Taffy put down her dessert spoon and looked at me curiously. "I didn't know the ARM took kidnapping cases."

"We don't. Kidnapping would be a regional problem. Bera thought—" I stopped, because Chambers looked around suddenly, right at me. He seemed surprised and annoyed.

I hadn't realized how rudely I was staring. I looked away, embarrassed. "Bera thought an organlegging gang might be involved. Some of the gangs turned to kidnapping about that time, after the Freezer Law slid their markets out from under them. Is Chambers still looking at me?" I felt his eyes on the back of my neck.

"Yah."

"I wonder why."

"*Do* you indeed." Taffy knew, the way she was grinning. She gave me another two seconds of suspense, then said, "You're doing the cigarette trick."

"Oh. Right." I transferred the cigarette to a hand of flesh and blood. It's silly to forget how startling that can be: a cigarette or a pencil or a jigger of bourbon floating in mid-air. I've used it myself for shock effect.

Taffy said, "He's been in the boob cube a lot lately. He's the number eight corpsicle heir, worldwide. Didn't you know?"

"Corpsicle heir?"

"You know what *corpsicle* means? When the freezer vaults first opened—"

"I know. I didn't know they'd started using the word again."

"Well, never mind *that*. The *point* is that if the second Freezer Bill passes, about three hundred thousand corpsicles will be declared formally dead. Some of those frozen dead men have money. The money will go to their next of kin."

"*Oh*. And Chambers has an ancestor in a vault somewhere, does he?"

"Somewhere in Michigan. He's got an odd, Biblical name."

"Not Leviticus Hale?"

She stared. "Now, just how the bleep did you know that?"

"Just a stab in the dark." I didn't know what had made me say it. Leviticus Hale, dead, had a memorable face and a memorable name.

Strange, though, that I'd never thought of money as a motive for the second Freezer Bill. The first Freezer Law had applied only to the destitute, the Freezeout Kids.

Here are people who could not possibly adjust to any time in which they might be revived. They couldn't even adjust to their own times. Most of them weren't even sick, they didn't have that much excuse for foisting themselves on a nebulous future. Often they paid each other's way into the Freezer Vaults. If revived they would be paupers, unemployable, uneducated by any possible present or future standards; permanent malcontents.

Young, healthy, useless to themselves and society. And the organ banks are always empty . . .

The arguments for the second Freezer Bill were not much different. The corpsicles named in group two had money, but they were insane. Today there were chemical cures for most forms of insanity. But the memory of having been insane, the habitual thought patterns formed by paranoia or schizophrenia, these would remain, these would require psychotherapy. And how to cure them, in men and women whose patterns of experience were up to a hundred and forty years out of date to start with?

And the organ banks are always empty . . . Sure, I could see it. The citizens wanted to live forever. One day they'd work their way down to me, Gil Hamilton.

"You can't win," I said.

Taffy said, "How so?"

"If you're destitute they won't revive you because you

can't support yourself. If you're rich your heirs want the money. It's hard to defend yourself when you're dead."

"Everyone who loved them is dead too." She looked too seriously into her coffee cup. "I didn't really pay much attention when they passed the Freezer Law. At the hospital we don't even know where the spare parts come from: criminals, corpsicles, captured organleggers' stocks, it all looks the same. Lately I find myself wondering."

Taffy had once finished a lung transplant with hands and sterile steel, after the hospital machines had quit at an embarrassing moment. A squeamish woman couldn't have done that. But the transplants themselves had started to bother her lately. Since she met me. A surgeon and an organlegger-hunting ARM, we made a strange pairing.

When I looked again, Holden Chambers was gone. We split the tab, paid and left.

The first shopping level had an odd outdoor-indoor feel to it. We came out into a broad walk lined with shops and trees and theaters and sidewalk cafés, under a flat concrete sky forty feet up and glowing with light. Far away, an undulating black horizon showed in a narrow band between concrete sky and firmament.

The crowds had gone, but in some of the sidewalk cafés a few citizens still watched the world go by. We walked toward the black band of horizon, holding hands, taking our time. There was no way to hurry Taffy when she was passing shop windows. All I could do was stop when she did, wearing or not wearing an indulgent smile. Jewelry, clothing, all glowing behind plate glass—

She tugged my arm, turning sharply to look into a furniture store. I don't know what it was she saw. I saw a dazzling pulse of green light on the glass, and a puff of green flame spurting from a coffee table.

Very strange. Surrealistic, I thought. Then the impressions sorted out, and I pushed Taffy hard in the small of the back and flung myself rolling in the opposite direction. Green light flashed briefly, very near. I stopped rolling. There was a weapon in my sporran the size of a double barreled Derringer, two compressed air cartridges firing clusters of anesthetic crystal slivers.

A few puzzled citizens had stopped to watch what I was doing.

I ripped my sporran apart with both hands. Everything spilled out, rolling coins and credit cards and ARM ident and cigarettes and—I snatched up the ARM weapon. The window reflection had been a break. Usually you can't tell *where* the pulse from a hunting laser might have come from.

Green light flashed near my elbow. The pavement cracked loudly and peppered me with particles. I fought an urge to fling myself backward. The afterimage was on my retina, a green line thin as a razor's edge, pointing right at him.

He was in a cross street, posed kneeling, waiting for his gun to pulse again. I sent a cloud of mercy needles toward him. He slapped at his face, turned to run, and fell skidding.

I stayed where I was.

Taffy was curled in the pavement with her head buried in her arms. There was no blood around her. When I saw her legs shift I knew she wasn't dead. I still didn't know if she'd been hit.

Nobody else tried to shoot at us.

The man with the gun lay where he was for almost a minute. Then he started twitching.

He was in convulsions when I got to him. Mercy needles aren't supposed to do that. I got his tongue out of his throat so he couldn't choke, but I wasn't carrying medicines that could help. When the High Cliffs police arrived, he was dead.

Inspector Swan was a picture-poster cop, tri-racial and handsome as hell in an orange uniform that seemed tailored to him, so well did he fit it. He had the gun open in front of him and was probing at the electronic guts of it with a pair of tweezers. He said, "You don't have any idea why he was shooting at you?"

"That's right."

"You're an ARM. What do you work on these days?"

"Organlegging, mostly. Tracking down gangs that have gone into hiding." I was massaging Taffy's neck and shoulders, trying to calm her down. She was still shivering. The muscles under my hands were very tight.

Swan frowned. "Such an easy answer. But he couldn't be part of an organlegging gang, could he? Not with that gun."

"True." I ran my thumbs around the curve of Taffy's shoulder blades. She reached around and squeezed my hand.

The gun. I hadn't really expected Swan to see the implications. It was an unmodified hunting laser, right off the rack.

Officially, nobody in the world makes guns to kill people. Under the Conventions, not even armies use them, and the United Nations police use mercy weapons, with the intent that the criminals concerned should be unharmed for trial—and, later, for the organ banks. The only killing weapons made are for killing animals. They are supposed to be, well, sportsmanlike.

A continuous-firing X-ray laser would be easy enough to make. It would chop down anything living, no matter how fast it fled, no matter what it hid behind. The beast wouldn't even know it was being shot at until you waved the beam through its body: an invisible sword blade a mile long.

But that's butchery. The prey should have a chance; it should at least know it's being shot at. A standard hunting laser fires a pulse of visible light, and won't fire again for about a second. It's no better than a rifle, except in that you don't have to allow for windage, the range is close enough to infinite, you can't run out of bullets, it doesn't mess up the meat, and there's no recoil. That's what makes it sportsmanlike.

Against me it had been just sportsmanlike enough. He was dead. I wasn't.

"Not that it's so censored easy to modify a hunting laser," said Swan. "It takes some basic electronics. I could do it myself—"

"So could I. Why not? We've both had police training."

"The point is, I don't *know* anyone who couldn't *find* someone to modify a hunting laser, give it a faster pulse or even a continuous beam. Your friend must have been afraid to bring anyone else into it. He must have had a very personal grudge against you. You're sure you don't recognize him?"

"I never saw him before. Not with *that* face."

"And he's dead," said Swan.

"That doesn't really prove anything. Some people have allergic reactions to police anesthetics."

"You used a standard ARM weapon?"

"Yah. I didn't even fire both barrels. I *couldn't* have put a *lot* of needles in him. But there are allergic reactions."

"Especially if you take something to bring them on." Swan put the gun down and stood up. "Now, I'm just a city cop, and I don't know that much about ARM business. But I've heard that organleggers sometimes take something so they won't just go to sleep when an ARM anesthetic hits them."

"Yah. Organleggers don't like becoming spare parts themselves. I do have a theory, Inspector."

"Try me."

"He's a retired organlegger. A lot of them retired when the Freezer Bill passed. Their markets were gone, and they'd made their pile, some of them. They split up and became honest citizens. A respected citizen may keep a hunting laser on his wall, but it isn't modified. He could modify it if he had to, with a day's notice."

"Then said respected citizen spotted an old enemy."

"Going into a restaurant, maybe. And he just had time to go home for his gun, while we ate dinner."

"Sounds reasonable. How do we check it?"

"If you'll do a rejection spectrum on his brain tissue, and send everything you've got to ARM Headquarters, we'll do the rest. An organlegger can change his face and fingerprints as he censored pleases, but he can't change his tolerance to transplants. Chances are he's on record."

"And you'll let me know."

"Right."

Swan was checking it with the radio on his scooter while I beeped my clicker for a taxi. The taxi settled at the edge of the walkway. I helped Taffy into it. Her movements were slow and jerky. She wasn't in shock, just depression.

Swan called from his scooter. "Hamilton!"

I stopped halfway into the taxi. "Yah?"

"He's a local," Swan boomed. His voice carried like an orator's. "Mortimer Lincoln, ninety-fourth floor. Been living here since—" He checked again with his radio. "April, 2123. I'd guess that's about six months after they passed the Freezer Law."

"Thanks." I typed an address on the cab's destination board. The cab hummed and rose.

I watched High Cliffs recede, a pyramid as big as a mountain, glowing with light. The city guarded by Inspector Swan was all in one building. It would make his job easier, I thought. Society would be a bit more organized.

Taffy spoke for the first time in a good while. "Nobody's ever shot at me before."

"It's all over now. I think he was shooting at me anyway."

"I suppose." Suddenly she was shaking. I took her in my arms and held her. She talked into my shirt collar. "I didn't know what was happening. That green light, I thought it was *pretty*. I didn't know what happened until you knocked me down, and then that green line flashed at you and I heard the sidewalk go *ping,* and I didn't know what to *do!* I—"

"You did fine."

"I wanted to *help!* I didn't know, maybe you were dead, and there wasn't anything I could do. If you hadn't had a gun—Do you always carry a gun?"

"Always."

"I never knew." Without moving, she seemed to pull away from me a little.

At one time the Amalgamation of Regional Militia had been a federation of Civil Defense bodies in a number of nations. Later it had become the police force of the United Nations itself. They had kept the name. Probably they liked the acronym.

When I got to the office the next morning, Jackson Bera had already run the dead man to Earth. "No question about it," he told me. "His rejection spectrum checks perfectly. Anthony Tiller, known organlegger, suspected member of the Anubis gang. First came on the scene around 2120; he probably had another name and face before that. Disappeared April or May 2123."

"That fits. No, dammit, it doesn't. He must have been out of his mind. There he was, home free, rich and safe. Why would he blow it all to kill a man who never harmed a hair of his head?"

"You don't *really* expect an organlegger to behave like a well-adjusted member of society." -

I answered Bera's grin. "I guess not . . . Hey. You said *Anubis*, didn't you? The Anubis gang, not the Loren gang."

"That's what it says on the hard copy. Shall I query for probability?"

"Please." Bera programs a computer better than I do. I talked while he tapped at the keyboard in my desk. "Whoever the bleep he was, Anubis controlled the illicit medical facilities over a big section of the Midwest. Loren had a piece of the North American west coast, smaller area, bigger population. The difference is that I killed Loren myself, by squeezing the life out of his heart with my imaginary hand, which is a very personal thing, as you will realize, Jackson. Whereas I never touched Anubis or any of his gang, nor even interfered with his profits, to the best of my knowledge."

"I did," said Bera. "Maybe he thought I was you." Which is hilarious, because Bera is dark brown and a foot taller than me if you include the hair that puffs out around his head like a black powder explosion. "You missed something. Anubis was an intriguing character. He changed faces and ears and fingerprints whenever he got the urge. We're pretty sure he was male, but even that isn't worth a big bet. He's changed his height at least once. Full leg transplant."

"Loren couldn't do that. Loren was a pretty sick boy. He probably went into organlegging because he needed the transplant supply."

"Not Anubis. Anubis must have had a sky-high rejection threshold."

"Jackson, *you're proud of Anubis.*"

Bera was shocked to his core. "The hell! He's a dirty murdering organlegger! If I'd *caught* him I'd be proud of Anubis—" He stopped, because my desk screen was getting information.

The computer in the basement of the ARM building

gave Anthony Tiller no chance at all of being part of the Loren gang, and a probability in the nineties that he had run with the Jackal God. One point was that Anubis and the rest had all dropped out of sight around the end of April, 2123, when Anthony Tiller/Mortimer Lincoln changed his face and moved into High Cliffs.

"It could still have been revenge," Bera suggested. "Loren and Anubis knew each other. We know that much. They set up the boundary between their territories at least twelve years ago, by negotiation. Loren took over Anubis' territory when Anubis retired. And you killed Loren."

I scoffed. "And Tiller the Killer gave up his cover to get me, two years after the gang broke up?"

"Maybe it wasn't revenge. Maybe Anubis wants to make a comeback."

"Or maybe this Tiller just flipped. Withdrawal symptoms. He hadn't killed anyone for almost two years, poor baby. I wish he'd picked a better time."

"Why?"

"Taffy was with me. She's still twitching."

"You didn't tell me that! She wasn't hit, was she?"

"No, just scared."

Bera relaxed. His hand caressed the interface where his hair faded into air, feather-lightly, in the nervous way another man might scratch his head. "I'd hate to see you two split up."

"Oh, it's not . . ." anything like that serious, I'd have told him, but he knew better. "Yah. We didn't get much sleep last night. It isn't just being shot at, you know."

"I know."

"Taffy's a surgeon. She thinks of transplant stocks as raw material. Tools. She'd be crippled without an organ bank. She doesn't think of the stuff as human . . . or she never used to, till she met me."

"I've never heard either of you talk about it."

"We don't, even to each other, but it's there. Most transplants are condemned criminals, captured by heroes such as you and me. Some of the stuff is respectable citizens captured by organleggers, broken up into illicit organ banks and eventually recaptured by said heroes. They don't tell Taffy which is which. She works with pieces of people. I don't think she can live with me and not live with that."

"Getting shot at by an ex-organlegger couldn't have helped much. We'd better see to it that it doesn't happen again."

"Jackson, he was just a nut."

"He used to be with Anubis."

"I never had anything to do with Anubis." Which reminded me. "You did, though, didn't you? Do you remember anything about the Holden Chambers kidnapping?"

Bera looked at me peculiarly. "Holden and Charlotte Chambers, yah. You've got a good memory. There's a fair chance Anubis was involved."

"Tell me about it."

"There was a rash of kidnappings about that time, all over the world. You know how organlegging works. The legitimate hospitals are always short of transplants. Some sick citizens are too much in a hurry to wait their turns. The gangs kidnap a healthy citizen, break him up into spare parts, throw away the brain, use the rest for illegal operations. That's the way it was until the Freezer Law cut the market out from under them."

"I remember."

"Some gangs turned to kidnapping for ransom. Why not? It's just what they were set up for. If the family couldn't pay off, the victim could always become a donor. It made people much more likely to pay off.

"The only strange thing about the Chambers kidnap was that Holden and Charlotte Chambers both disappeared about the same time, around six at night." Bera had been tapping at the computer controls. He looked at the screen and said, "Make that seven. March 21, 2123. But they were miles apart, Charlotte at a restaurant with a date, Holden at Washburn University attending a night class. Now why would a kidnap gang think they needed them both?"

"Any ideas?"

"They might have thought that the Chambers trustees were more likely to pay off on both of them. We'll never know now. We never got any of the kidnappers. We were lucky to get the kids back."

"What made you think it was Anubis?"

"It was Anubis territory. The Chambers kidnap was only the last of half a dozen in that area. Smooth operations, no excitement, no hitches, victims returned intact after the ransom was paid." He glared. "No, I'm *not* proud of Anubis. It's just that he tended not to make mistakes, and he was used to making people disappear."

"Uh huh."

"They made themselves disappear, the whole gang, around the time of that last kidnap. We assume they were building up a stake."

"How much did they get?"

"On the Chambers kids? A hundred thousand."

"They'd have made ten times that selling them as transplants. They must have been hard up."

"You know it. Nobody was buying. What does all this have to do with your being shot at?"

"A wild idea. Could Anubis be interested in the Chambers kids *again?*"

Bera gave me a funny look. "No way. What for? They bled them white the first time. A hundred thousand UN marks isn't play money."

After Bera left I sat there not believing it.

Anubis had vanished. Loren had acted immediately to take over Anubis' territory. Where had they gone, Anubis and the others? Into Loren's organ banks?

But there was Tiller/Lincoln.

I didn't *like* the idea that any random ex-organlegger might decide to kill me the instant he saw me. Finally I did something about it. I asked the computer for data on the Chambers kidnapping.

There wasn't much Bera hadn't told me. I wondered, though, why he hadn't mentioned Charlotte's condition.

When ARM police found the Chambers kids drugged on a hotel parking roof, they had both been in good physical condition. Holden had been a little scared, a little relieved, just beginning to get angry. But Charlotte had been in catatonic withdrawal. At last notice she was still in catatonic withdrawal. She had never spoken with coherence about the kidnapping, nor about anything else.

Something had been done to her. Something terrible. Maybe Bera had taught himself not to think about it. Otherwise the kidnappers had behaved almost with rectitude. The ransom had been paid, the victims had been returned. They had been on that roof, drugged, for less than twenty minutes. They showed no bruises, no signs of maltreatment . . . another sign that their kidnappers were organleggers. Organleggers aren't sadists. They don't have that much respect for the stuff.

I noted that the ransom had been paid by an attorney. The Chambers kids were orphans. If they'd both been killed the executor of their estate would have been out of a job. From that viewpoint it made sense to capture them both . . . but not all *that* much sense.

And there couldn't be a motive for kidnapping them again. They didn't have the money. Except—

It hit me joltingly. *The second Freezer Bill.*

Holden Chambers' number was in the basement computer. I was dialing it when second thoughts interrupted. Instead I called downstairs and set a team to locating possible bugs in Chambers' home or phone. They weren't to interfere with the bugs or to alert possible listeners. Routine stuff.

Once before the Chambers kids had disappeared. If we weren't lucky they might disappear again. Sometimes the ARM business was like digging a pit in quicksand. If you dug hard enough you could maintain a noticeable depression, but as soon as you stopped . . .

The Freezer Law of 2122 had given the ARM a field day. Some of the gangs had simply retired. Some had tried to keep going, and wound up selling an operation to an ARM plant. Some had tried to reach other markets; but there weren't any, not even for Loren, who had tried to expand into the asteroid belt and found they wouldn't have him either.

And some had tried kidnapping; but inexperience kept tripping them up. The name of a victim points straight at a kidnapper's only possible market. Too often the ARMs had been waiting.

We'd cleaned them out. Organlegging should have been an extinct profession this past year. The vanished jackals I spent my days hunting should have posed no present threat to society.

Except that the legitimate transplants released by the Freezer Law were running out. And a peculiar thing was happening. People had started to disappear from stalled vehicles, singles apartment houses, crowded city slide-walks.

Earth wanted the organleggers back.

No, that wasn't fair. Put it this way: enough citizens wanted to extend their own lives, at any cost . . .

If Anubis was alive, he might well be thinking of going back into business.

The point was that he would need backing. Loren had taken over his medical facilities when Anubis retired. Eventually we'd located those and destroyed them. Anubis would have to start over.

Let the second Freezer Bill pass, and Leviticus Hale would be spare parts. Charlotte and Holden Chambers would inherit . . . how much?

I got that via a call to the local NBA news depart-ment. In one hundred and thirty-four years Leviticus Hale's original three hundred and twenty thousand dol-lars had become seventy-five million UN marks.

I spent the rest of the morning on routine. They call it *legwork*, though it's mostly done by phone and comput-er keyboard. The word covers some unbelievable long shots.

We were investigating every member of every Citi-zen's Committee to Oppose the Second Freezer Bill in the world. The suggestion had come down from old man Garner. He thought we might find that a coalition of or-ganleggers had pooled advertising money to keep the corpsicles off the market. The results that morning didn't look promising.

I half hoped it wouldn't work out. Suppose those committees *did* turn out to be backed by organleggers? It would make prime time news, anywhere in the world. The second Freezer Bill would pass like *that*. But it had to be checked. There had been opposition to the first Freezer Bill, too, when the gangs had had more money.

Money. We spent a good deal of computer time look-ing for unexplained money. The average criminal tends to think that once he's got the money, he's home free, the game is over.

We hadn't caught a sniff of Loren or Anubis that way.

Where had Anubis spent his money? Maybe he'd just hidden it away somewhere, or maybe Loren had killed him for it. And Tiller had shot at me because he didn't like my face. Legwork is gambling, time against results.

It developed that Holden Chambers' environs were free of eavesdropping devices. I called him about noon.

There appeared within my phone screen a red-faced, white-haired man of great dignity. He asked to whom I wished to speak. I told him, and displayed my ARM ident. He nodded and put me on hold.

Moments later I faced a weak-chinned young man who smilled distractedly at me and said, "Sorry about that. I've been getting considerable static from the news lately. Zero acts as a kind of, ah, buffer."

Past his shoulder I could see a table with things on it: a tape viewer, a double handful of tape spools, a tape recorder the size of a man's palm, two pens and a stack of paper, all neatly arranged. I said, "Sorry to interrupt your studying."

"That's all right. It's tough getting back to it after Year's-End. Maybe you remember. Haven't I seen you —? *Oh.* The floating cigarette."

"That's right."

"How did you do that?"

"I've got an imaginary arm." And it's a great conversational device, an ice-breaker of wondrous potency. I was a marvel, a talking sea serpent, the way the kid was looking at me. "I lost an arm once, mining rocks in the Belt. A sliver of asteroidal rock sheared it off clean to the shoulder."

He looked awed.

"I got it replaced, of course. But for a year I was a one-armed man. Well, here was a whole section of my brain developed to control a right arm, and no right arm. Psychokinesis is easy enough to develop when you live in a low-gravity environment." I paused just less than long enough for him to form a question. "Somebody tried to kill me outside Midgard last night. That's why I called."

I hadn't expected him to burst into a fit of the giggles. "Sorry," he got out. "It sounds like you lead an active life!"

"Yah. It didn't seem that funny at the time. I don't suppose you noticed anything unusual last night?"

"Just the usual shootings and muggings, and there was one guy with a cigarette floating in front of his face." He sobered before my clearly deficient sense of humor. "Look, I *am* sorry, but one minute you're talking about a meteor shearing your arm off, and the next it's bullets whizzing past your ear."

"Sure, I see your point."

"I left before you did. I know censored well I did. What happened?"

"Somebody shot at us with a hunting laser. He was probably just a nut. He was also part of the gang that kidnapped—" He looked stricken. "Yah, them. There's probably no connection, but we wondered if you might have noticed anything. Like a familiar face."

He shook his head. "They change faces, don't they?"

"Usually. How did you leave?"

"Taxi. I live in Bakersfield, about twenty minutes from High Cliffs. Where did all this happen? I caught my taxi on the third shopping level."

"That kills it. We were on the first."

"I'm not really sorry. He might have shot at me too."

I'd been trying to decide whether to tell him that the kidnap gang might be interested in him again. Whether to scare the lights out of him on another long shot, or leave him off guard for a possible kidnap attempt. He seemed stable enough, but you never knew.

I temporized. "Mister Chambers, we'd like you to try to identify the man who tried to kill me last night. He probably did change his face—"

"Yah." He was uneasy. Many citizens would be, if asked to look a dead man in the face. "But I suppose you've got to try it. I'll stop in tomorrow afternoon, after class."

So. Tomorrow we'd see what he was made of.

He asked, "What about that imaginary arm? I've never heard of a psi talking that way about his talent."

"I wasn't being cute," I told him. "It's an arm, as far as I'm concerned. My limited imagination. I can feel things out with my fingertips, but not if they're further away than an arm can reach. A jigger of bourbon is about the biggest thing I can lift. Most psis can't do near-ly that well."

"But they can reach further. Why not try a hypno-tist?"

"And lose the whole arm? I don't want to risk that."

He looked disappointed in me. "What can you do with an imaginary arm that you can't do with a real one?"

"I can pick up hot things without burning myself."

"*Yah!*" He hadn't thought of that.

"And I can reach through walls. [In the Belt I could reach through my suit and do precision work in vacuum.] I can reach *two* ways through a phone screen. Fiddle with the works, or—here, I'll show you."

It doesn't always work. But I was getting a good pic-ture. Chambers showed life-sized; in color and stereo, through four square feet of screen. It looked like I could reach right into it. So I did. I reached into the screen with my imaginary hand, picked a pencil off the table in front of him and twirled it like a baton.

He threw himself backward out of his chair. He land-ed rolling. I saw his face, pale gray with terror, before he rolled away and out of view. A few seconds later the screen went blank. He must have turned the knob from off-screen.

If I'd touched his face I could have understood it. But all I'd done was lift a pencil. What the hell?

My fault, I guessed. Some people see psi powers as supernatural, eerie, threatening. I shouldn't have been showing off like that. But Holden hadn't looked the type. Brash, a bit nervous, but fascinated rather than re-pulsed by the possibilities of an invisible, immaterial hand.

Then, terror.

I didn't try to call him back. I dithered about putting a guard on him, decided not to. A guard might be no-ticed. But I ordered a tracer implanted in him.

Anubis might pick Chambers up at any time. He needn't wait for the General Assembly to declare Leviti-cus Hale dead.

A tracer needle was a useful thing. It would be fired at Chambers from ambush. He'd probably never notice the sting, the hole would be only a pinprick, and it would tell us just where he was from then on.

I thought Charlotte Chambers could use a tracer too, so I picked up a palm-size pressure implanter downstairs. I also traded the discharged barrel on my sidearm for a fresh one. The feel of the gun in my hand sent vivid green lines sizzling past my mind's eye.

Last, I ordered a standard information package, C priority, on what Chambers had been doing for the last two years. It would probably arrive in a day or so.

The winter face of Kansas had great dark gaps in it, a town nestled in each gap. The weather domes of various townships had shifted kilotons of snow outward, to deepen the drifts across the flat countryside. In the light of early sunset the snowbound landscape was orange-white, striped with the broad black shadows of a few cities-within-buildings. It all seemed eerie and abstract, sliding west beneath the folded wings of our plane.

We slowed hard in midair. The wings unfolded, and we settled over downtown Topeka.

This was going to look odd on my expense account. All this way to see a girl who hadn't spoken sense in three years. Probably it would be disallowed . . . yet she was as much a part of the case as her brother. Anyone planning to recapture Holden Chambers for reransom would want Charlotte too.

Menninger Institute was a pretty place. Besides the twelve stories of glass and mock-brick which formed the main building, there were at least a dozen outbuildings of varied ages and designs that ran from boxlike rectangles to free-form organics poured in foam plastic. They were all wide apart, separated by green lawns and trees and flower beds. A place of peace, a place with elbow room. Pairs and larger groups passed me on the curving walks: an aide and a patient, or an aide and several less disturbed patients. The aides were obvious at a glance.

"When a patient is well enough to go outside for a walk, then he needs the greenery and the room," Doctor Hartman told me. "It's part of his therapy. Going outside is a giant step."

"Do you get many agoraphobes?"

"No, that's not what I was talking about. It's the *lock* that counts. To anyone else that lock is a prison, but to many patients it comes to represent security. Someone else to make the decisions, to keep the world outside."

Doctor Hartman was short and round and blond. A comfortable person, easy-going, patient, sure of himself. Just the man to trust with your destiny, assuming you were tired of running it yourself.

I asked, "Do you get many cures?"

"Certainly. As a matter of fact, we generally won't take patients unless we feel we can cure them."

"That must do wonders for the record."

He was not offended. "It does even more for the patients. Knowing that we know they can be cured makes them feel the same way. And the incurably insane . . . can be damned depressing." Momentarily he seemed to sag under an enormous weight. Then he was himself again. "They can affect the other patients. Fortunately there aren't many incurables, these days."

"Was Charlotte Chambers one of the curables?"

"We thought so. After all, it was only shock. There was no previous history of personality disturbances. Her blood psychochemicals were near enough normal. We tried everything in the records. Stroking. Fiddling with her chemistry. Psychotherapy didn't get very far. Either she's deaf or she doesn't listen, and she won't talk. Sometimes I think she hears everything we say . . . but she doesn't respond."

We had reached a powerful-looking locked door. Doctor Hartman searched through a key ring, touched a key to the lock. "We call it the violent ward, but it's more properly the severely disturbed ward. I wish to hell we *could* get some violence out of some of them. Like Charlotte. They won't even *look* at reality, much less try to fight it . . . here we are."

Her door opened outward into the corridor. My nasty professional mind tagged the fact: if you tried to hang yourself from the door, anyone could see you from either end of the corridor. It would be very public.

In these upper rooms the windows were frosted. I suppose there's good reason why some patients shouldn't be reminded that they are twelve stories up. The room was small but well lighted and brightly painted, with a bed and a padded chair and a tridee screen set flush with the wall. There wasn't a sharp corner anywhere in the room.

Charlotte was in the chair, looking straight ahead of her, her hands folded in her lap. Her hair was short and not particularly neat. Her yellow dress was of some wrinkleproof fabric. She looked resigned, I thought, resigned to some ultimately awful thing. She did not notice us as we came in.

I whispered, "Why is she still here, if you can't cure her?"

Doctor Hartman spoke in a normal tone. "At first we thought it was catatonic withdrawal. That we could have cured. This isn't the first time someone has suggested moving her. She's still here because I want to know what's *wrong* with her. She's been like this ever since they brought her in."

She still hadn't noticed us. The doctor talked as if she couldn't hear us. "Do the ARMs have any idea what was done to her? If we knew that we might be better able to treat her."

I shook my head. "I was going to ask you. What *could* they have done to her?"

He shook his head.

"Try another angle, then. What couldn't they have done to her? There were no bruises, broken bones, anything like that—"

"No internal injuries either. No surgery was performed on her. There was the evidence of drugging. I understand they were organleggers?"

"It looks likely." She could have been pretty, I thought. It wasn't the lack of cosmetics, or even the gaunt look. It was the empty eyes, isolated above high cheekbones, looking at nothing. "Could she be blind?"

"No. The optic nerves function perfectly."

She reminded me of a wirehead. You can't get a wirehead's attention either, when house current is trickling down a fine wire from the top of his skull into the pleasure center of his brain. But no, the pure egocentric joy of a wirehead hardly matched Charlotte's egocentric misery.

"Tell me," said Doctor Hartman. "How badly could an organlegger frighten a young girl?"

"We don't get many citizens back from organleggers. I . . . honestly can't think of any upper limit. They could have taken her on a tour of the medical facilities. They could have made her watch while they broke up a prospect for stuff." I didn't like what my imagination was doing. There are things you don't think about, because the point is to protect the prospects, keep the Lorens and the Anubises from reaching them at all. But you can't help thinking about them anyway, so you push them back, push them back. These things must have been in my head for a long time. "They had the facilities to partly break her up and put her back together again and leave her conscious the whole time. You wouldn't have found scars. The only scars they can't cure with modern medicine are in the bone itself. They could have done any kind of temporary transplant—and they must have been bored, Doctor. Business was slow. But—"

"Stop." He was gray around the edges. His voice was weak and hoarse.

"But organleggers aren't sadists, generally. They don't have that much respect for the stuff. They wouldn't play that kind of game unless they had something special against her."

"My God, you play rough games. How can you sleep nights, knowing what you know?"

"None of your business, Doctor. In your opinion, is it likely that she was frightened into this state?"

"Not all at once. We could have brought her out of it if it had happened all at once. I suppose she may have been frightened repeatedly. How long did they have her?"

"Nine days."

Hartman looked worse yet. Definitely he was not ARM material.

I dug in my sporran for the pressure implanter. "I'd like your permission to put a tracer needle in her. I won't hurt her."

"There's no need to whisper, Mr. Hamilton—"

"Was I?" Yes, dammit, I'd been holding my voice low, as if I were afraid to disturb her. In a normal voice I said, "The tracer could help us locate her in case she disappears."

"Disappears? Why should she do that? You can see for yourself—"

"That's the worst of it. The same gang of organleggers that got her the first time may be trying to kidnap her again. Just how good is your . . . security . . ." I trailed off. Charlotte Chambers had turned around and was looking at me.

Hartman's hand closed hard on my upper arm. He was warning me. Calmly, reassuringly, he said, "Don't worry, Charlotte. I'm Doctor Hartman. You're in good hands. We'll take care of you."

Charlotte was half out of her chair, twisted around to search my face. I tried to look harmless. Naturally I knew better than to try to guess what she was thinking. Why should her eyes be big with hope? Frantic, desperate hope. When I'd just uttered a terrible threat.

Whatever she was looking for, she didn't find it in my face. What looked like hope gradually died out of her eyes, and she sank back in her chair, looking straight ahead of her, without interest. Doctor Hartman gestured, and I took the hint and left.

Twenty minutes later he joined me in the visitor's waiting room. "Hamilton, that's the first time she's ever shown that much awareness. What could possibly have sparked it?"

I shook my head. "I wanted to ask, just how good is your security?"

"I'll warn the aides. We can refuse to permit her visitors unless accompanied by an ARM agent. Is that good enough?"

"It may be, but I want to plant a tracer in her. Just in case."

"All right."

"Doctor, what was that in her expression?"

"I thought it was hope. Hamilton, I will just bet it was your voice that did it. You may sound like someone she knows. Let me take a recording of your voice and we'll see if we can find a psychiatrist who sounds like you."

When I put the tracer in her, she never so much as twitched.

All the way home her face haunted me. As if she'd waited two years in that chair, not bothering to move or think, until I came. Until finally I came.

My right side seems weightless. It throws me off
stride as I back away, back away. My right arm ends at
the shoulder. Where my left eye was is an empty socket.
Something vague shuffles out of the dark, looks at me
with its one left eye, reaches for me with its one right
arm. I back away, back away, fending it off with my
imaginary arm. It comes closer, I touch it, I reach into it.
Horrible! The scars! Loren's pleural cavity is a patch-
work of transplants. I want to snatch my hand away. Instead I reach deeper, and find his borrowed heart, and
squeeze. And squeeze.

How can I sleep nights, knowing what I know? Well,
Doctor, some nights I dream.

Taffy opened her eyes to find me sitting up in bed,
staring at a dark wall. She said, "What?"

"Bad dream."

"Oh." She scratched me under the ear, for reassur-
ance.

"How awake are you?"

She sighed. "Wide awake."

"Corpsicle. Where did you hear the word *corpsicle*?
In the boob cube? From a friend?"

"I don't remember. Why?"

"Just a thought. Never mind. I'll ask Luke Garner."

I got up and made us some hot chocolate with bourbon flavoring. It knocked us out like a cluster of mercy
needles.

Lucas Garner was a man who had won a gamble with
fate. Medical technology had progressed as he grew older, so that his expected lifespan kept moving ahead of
him. He was not yet the oldest living member of the
Struldbrugs' Club, but he was getting on, getting on.

His spinal nerves had worn out long since, marooning
him in a ground-effect travel chair. His face hung loose
from his skull, in folds. But his arms were apishly
strong, and his brain still worked. He was my boss.

"Corpsicle," he said. "Corpsicle. Right. They've been
saying it on tridee. I didn't notice, but you're right. It's
funny they should start using that word again."

"How did it get started?"

"Popsicle. A popsicle was frozen sherbet on a stick. You licked it off."

I winced at the mental picture that evoked. Leviticus Hale, covered with frost, a stake up his anus, a gigantic tongue—

"A *wooden* stick." Garner had a grin to scare babies. Grinning, he was almost a work of art: an antique, a hundred and eighty-odd years old, like a Hannes Bok illustration of Lovecraft. "That's how long ago it was. They didn't start freezing people until the nineteen sixties or seventies, but we were still putting wooden sticks in popsicles. Why would anyone use it now?"

"Who uses it? Newscasters? I don't watch the boob cube much."

"Newscasters, yah, and lawyers . . . How are you making out on the Committees to Oppose the Second Freezer Bill?"

It took me a moment to make the switch. "No positive results. The program's still running, and results are slow in some parts of the world, Africa, the Middle East . . . They all seem to be solid citizens."

"Well, it's worth a try. We've been looking into the other side of it, too. If organleggers are trying to block the second Freezer Bill, they might well try to intimidate or kill off anyone who *backs* the second Freezer Bill. Follow me?"

"I suppose."

"So we have to know who to protect. It's strictly business, of course. The ARM isn't supposed to get involved in politics."

Garner reached sideways to tap one-handed at the computer keyboard in his desk. His bulky floating chair wouldn't fit under the keyboard. Tape slid from the slot, two feet of it. He handed it to me.

"Mostly lawyers," he said. "A number of sociologists and humanities professors. Religious leaders pushing their own brand of immortality; we've got religious factions on both sides of the question. These are the people who publicly back the second Freezer Bill. I'd guess they're the ones who started using the word *corpsicle.*"

"Thanks."

"Cute word, isn't it? A joke. If you said *frozen sleep* someone might take you seriously. Someone might even wonder if they were really dead. Which is the key question, isn't it? The corpsicles they want are the ones who were healthiest, the ones who have the best chance of being brought back to life some day. These are the people they want revived a piece at a time. By me that's lousy."

"Me too." I glanced down at the list. "I presume you haven't actually warned any of these people."

"No, you idiot. They'd go straight to a newscaster and tell him that all their opponents are organleggers."

I nodded. "Thanks for the help. If anything comes of this—"

"Sit down. Run your eyes down those names. See if you spot anything."

I didn't know most of them, of course, not even in the Americas. There were a few prominent defense lawyers, and at least one federal judge, and Raymond Sinclair the physicist, and a string of newscast stations, and—
"Clark and Nash? The advertising firm?"

"A number of advertising firms in a number of countries. Most of these people are probably sincere enough, and they'll talk to *anyone,* but the coverage has to come from somewhere. It's coming from these firms. That word *corpsicle has* to be an advertising stunt. The publicity on the corpsicle heirs: they may have had a hand in that too. You know about the corpsicle heirs?"

"Not a lot."

"NBA Broadcasting has been running down the heirs to the richest members of Group II, the ones who were committed to the freezer vaults for reasons that don't harm their value as—stuff." Garner spat the word. It was organlegger slang. "The paupers all went into the organ banks on the first Freezer Law, of course, so Group II boasts some considerable wealth. NBA found a few heirs who would never have turned up otherwise. I imagine a lot of them will be voting for the second Freezer Bill—"

"Yah."

"Only the top dozen have been getting the publicity. But it's still a powerful argument, isn't it? If the corpsicles are in frozen sleep, that's one thing. If they're *dead,* then people are being denied their rightful inheritance."

I asked the obvious question. "Who's paying for the advertising?"

"Now, we wondered about that. The firms wouldn't say. We dug a little further."

"And?"

"They don't know either." Garner grinned like Satan. "They were hired by firms that aren't listed anywhere. A number of firms, whose representatives only appeared once. They paid their fees in lump sums."

"It sounds like—no. They're on the wrong side."

"Right. Why would an organlegger be *pushing* the second Freezer Bill?"

I thought it over. "How about this? A number of old, sickly, wealthy men and women set up a fund to see to it that the public supply of spare parts isn't threatened. It's legal, at least; which dealling with an organlegger isn't. With enough of them it might even be cheaper."

"We thought of that. We're running a program on it. I've been asking some subtle questions around the Struldbrugs' Club, just because I'm a member. It has to be subtle. Legal it may be, but they wouldn't want publicity."

"No."

"And then I got your report this morning. Anubis and the Chambers kid, huh? Wouldn't it be nice if it went a bit further than that?"

"I don't follow you."

At this moment Garner looked like something that was ready to pounce. "Wouldn't it be wonderful if a federation of organleggers was backing the second Freezer Bill. The idea would be to kidnap *all* of the top corpsicle heirs *just before the Bill passes*. Most people worth kidnapping can afford to protect themselves. Guards, house alarms, wrist alarms. A corpsicle heir can't do that yet."

Garner leaned forward in his chair, doing the work with his arms. "If we could prove this, and give it some publicity, wouldn't it shoot hell out of the second Freezer Law?"

There was a memo on my desk when I got back. The data package on Holden Chambers was in the computer memory, waiting for me. I remembered that Holden

himself would be here this afternoon, unless the arm
trick had scared him off.

I punched for the package and read it through, trying
to decide just how sane the kid was. Most of the information had come from the college medical center.
They'd been worried about him too.

The kidnapping had interrupted his freshman year at
Washburn. His grades had dropped sharply afterward,
then sloped back to a marginal passing grade. In Sep-
tember he'd changed his major from architecture to
biochemistry. He'd made the switch easily. His grades
had been average or better during these last two years.

He lived alone, in one of those tiny apartments whose
furnishings are all memory plastic, extruded as needed.
Technology was cheaper than elbow room. The apartment house did have some communal facilities—sauna,
pool, cleaning robots, party room, room-service kitchen,
clothing dispensary . . . I wondered why he didn't get
a roommate. It would have saved him money, for one
thing. But his sex life had always been somewhat pas-
sive, and he'd never been gregarious, according to the
file. He'd just about pulled the hole in after him for
some months after the kidnapping. As if he'd lost all
faith in humanity.

If he'd been off the beam then, he seemed to have recovered. Even his sex life had improved. That information had not come from the the college medical center,
but from records from the communal kitchen (breakfast
for two, late night room service), and some recent recorded phone messages. All quite public; there was no
reason for me to be feeling like a peeping Tom. The
publicity on the corpsicle heirs may have done him
some good, started girls chasing him for a change. A few
had spent the night, but he didn't seem to be seeing anyone steadily.

I had wondered how he could afford a servant. The
answer had made me feel stupid. The secretary named Zero
turned out to be a computer construct, an answering
service.

Chambers was not penniless. After the ransom was
paid the trust fund had contained about twenty thousand
marks. Charlotte's care had eaten into that. The trustees
were giving Holden enough to pay his tuition and still

live comfortably. There would be some left when he graduated, but it would be earmarked for Charlotte.

I turned off the screen and thought about it. He'd had a jolt. He'd recovered. Some do, some don't. He'd been in perfect health, which has a lot to do with surviving emotional shock. If he was your friend today, you would avoid certain subjects in his presence.

And he'd thrown himself backward in blind terror when a pencil rose from his desk and started to pinwheel. How normal was that? I just didn't know. I was too used to my imaginary arm.

Holden himself appeared about fourteen hundred.

Anthony Tiller was in a cold box, face up. That face had been hideously contorted during his last minutes, but it showed none of that now. He was as expressionless as any dead man. The frozen sleepers at the Vault of Eternity had looked like that. Superficially, most of them had been in worse shape than he was.

Holden Chambers studied him with interest. "So that's what an organlegger looks like."

"An organlegger looks like anything he wants to."

He grimaced at that. He bent close to study the dead man's face. He circled the cold box with his hands clasped behind his back. He wanted to look nonchalant, but he was still walking wide of me. I didn't think the dead man bothered him.

He said the same thing I'd said two nights ago. "Nope. Not with that face."

"Well, it was worth a try. Let's go to my office. It's more comfortable."

He smiled. "Good."

He dawdled in the corridors. He looked into open offices, smiled at anyone who looked up, asked me mostly intelligent questions in a low voice. He was enjoying himself: a tourist in ARM Headquarters. But he trailed back when I tried to take the middle of the corridor, so that we wound up walking on opposite sides. Finally I asked him about it.

I thought he wasn't going to answer. Then, "It was that pencil trick."

"What about it?"

He sighed, as one who despairs of ever finding the

right words. "I don't like to be touched. I mean, I get along with girls all right, but generally I don't like to be touched."

"I didn't—"

"But you *could* have. And without my *knowing*. I couldn't see it, I might not even feel it. It just bothered the censored hell out of me, you reaching out of a phone screen like that! A phone call isn't supposed to be that, that *personal*." He stopped suddenly, looking down the corridor. "Isn't that Lucas Garner?"

"Yah."

"Lucas Garner!" He was awed and delighted. "He runs it all, doesn't he? How old is he now?"

"In his hundred and eighties." I thought of introducing him, but Luke's chair slid off in a different direction.

My office is just big enough for me, my desk, two chairs, and an array of spigots in the wall. I poured him tea and me coffee. I said, "I went to visit your sister."

"Charlotte? How is she?"

"I doubt she's changed since the last time you saw her. She doesn't notice anything around her . . . except for one incident, when she turned around and stared at me."

"Why? What did you do? What did you say?" he demanded.

Well, here it came. "I was telling her doctor that the same gang that kidnapped her once might want her again."

Strange things happened around his mouth. Bewilderment, fear, disbelief. "What the bleep made you say that?"

"It's a possibility. You're both corpsicle heirs. Tiller the Killer could have been watching you when he spotted *me* watching you. He couldn't have that."

"No, I suppose not . . ." He was trying to take it lightly, and he failed. "Do you seriously think they might want me—us—again?"

"It's a possibility," I repeated. "If Tiller was inside the restaurant, he could have spotted me by my floating cigarette. It's more distinctive than my face. Don't look so worried. We've got a tracer on you, we could track him anywhere he took you."

"In me?" He didn't like that much better—too personal?—but he didn't make an issue of it.

"Holden, I keep wondering what they could have done to your sister—"

He interrupted, coldly. "I stopped wondering that, long ago."

"—that they didn't do to you. It's more than curiosity. If the doctors knew what was done to her, if they knew what it is in her memory—"

"Dammit! Don't you think I want to help her? She's my sister!"

"All right." What was I playing psychiatrist for, anyway? Or was it detective I was playing? He didn't know anything. He was at the eye of several storms at once, and he must be getting sick and tired of it. I ought to send him home.

He spoke first. I could barely hear him. "You know what they did to me? A nerve block at the neck. A little widget taped to the back of my neck with surgical skin. I couldn't feel anything below the neck, and I couldn't move. They put that on me, dumped me on a bed and left me. For nine days. Every so often they'd turn me on again and let me drink and eat something and go to the bathroom."

"Did anyone tell you they'd break you up for stuff if they didn't get the ransom?"

He thought about it. "N-no. I could pretty well guess it. They never said anything to me at all. They treated me like I was dead. They examined me for, oh, it felt like hours, poking and prodding me with their hands and their instruments, rolling me around like dead meat. I couldn't feel any of it, but I could see it all. If they did that to Charlotte . . . maybe she thinks she's dead." His voice rose. "I've been through this again and again, with the ARMs, with Doctor Hartman, with the Washburn medical staff. Let's drop it, shall we?"

"Sure. I'm sorry. We don't learn tact in this business. We learn to ask questions. Any questions."

And yet, and yet, the look on her face.

I asked him one more question as I was escorting him out. Almost offhandedly. "What do you think of the second Freezer Bill?"

"I don't have a UN vote yet."

"That's not what I asked."

He faced me belligerently. "Look, there's a lot of money involved. A *lot* of money. It would pay for Charlotte the rest of her life. It would fix my face. But Hale, Leviticus Hale—" He pronounced the name accurately, and with no flicker of a smile. "He's a relative, isn't he? My great-to-the-third-grandfather. They could bring him back someday; it's possible. So what do I do? If I had a vote I'd have to decide. But I'm not twenty-five yet, so I don't have to worry about it."

"Interviews."

"I don't give interviews. You just got the same answer everyone else gets. It's on tape, on file with Zero. Goodbye, Mr. Hamilton."

Other ARM departments had thinned our ranks during the lull following the first Freezer Law. Over the next couple of weeks they began to trickle back. We needed operatives to implant tracers in unsuspecting victims, and afterward to monitor their welfare. We needed an augmented staff to follow their tracer blips on the screens downstairs.

We were sore tempted to tell all of the corpsicle heirs what was happening, and have them check in with us at regular intervals. Say, every fifteen minutes. It would have made things much easier. It might also have influenced their votes, altered the quality of the interviews they gave out.

But we didn't want to alert our quarry, the still hypothetical coalition of organleggers now monitoring the same corpsicle heirs we were interested in. And the backlash vote would be ferocious if we were wrong. And we weren't supposed to be interested in politics.

We operated without the knowledge of the corpsicle heirs. There were two thousand of them in all parts of the world, almost three hundred in the western United States, with an expected legacy of fifty thousand UN marks or more—a limit we set for our own convenience, because it was about all we could handle.

One thing helped the manpower situation. We had reached another lull. Missing persons complaints had dropped to near zero, all over the world.

"We should have been expecting that," Bera commented. "For the last year or so most of their customers must have stopped going to organleggers. They're waiting to see if the second Freezer Bill will go through. Now all the gangs are stuck with full organ banks and no customers. If they learned anything from last time, they'll pull in their horns and wait it out. Of course I'm only guessing—" But it looked likely enough. At any rate, we had the men we needed.

We monitored the top dozen corpsicle heirs twenty-four hours a day. The rest we checked at random intervals. The tracers could only tell us where they were, not who they were with or whether they wanted to be there. We had to keep checking to see if anyone had disappeared.

We sat back to await results.

The Security Council passed the second Freezer Bill on February 3, 2125. Now it would go to the world vote in late March. The voting public numbered ten billion, of whom perhaps sixty percent would bother to phone in their votes.

I took to watching the boob cube again.

NBA Broadcasting continued its coverage of the corpsicle heirs and its editorials in favor of the bill. Proponents took every opportunity to point out that many corpsicle heirs still remained to be discovered. (And YOU might be one.) Taffy and I watched a parade in New York in favor of the bill: banners and placards (SAVE THE LIVING, NOT THE DEAD . . . IT'S *YOUR* LIFE AT STAKE . . . CORPSICLES KEEP BEER COLD) and one censored big mob of chanting people. The transportation costs must have been formidable.

The various committees to oppose the bill were also active. In the Americas they pointed out that, although about forty percent of people in frozen sleep were in the Americas, the spare parts derived would go to the world at large. In Africa and Asia it was discovered that the Americas had most of the corpsicle heirs. In Egypt an analogy was made between the pyramids and the freezer vaults: both bids for immortality. It didn't go over well.

Polls indicated that the Chinese sectors would vote against the bill. NBA newscasters spoke of ancestor worship, and reminded the public that six ex-Chairmen resided in Chinese freezer vaults, alongside a myriad lesser ex-officials. Immortality was a respected tradition in China.

The committees to oppose reminded the world's voting public that some of the wealthiest of the frozen dead had heirs in the Belt. Were Earth's resources to be spread indiscriminately among the asteroidal rocks? I started to hate both sides. Fortunately the UN cut that line off fast by threatening injunction. Earth needed Belt resources too heavily.

Our own results began to come in.

Mortimer Lincoln, alias Anthony Tiller, had not been at Midgard the night he tried to kill me. He'd eaten alone in his apartment, a meal sent from the communal kitchen. Which meant that he himself could not have been watching Chambers.

We found no sign of anyone lurking behind Holden Chambers, or behind any of the other corpsicle heirs, publicized or not, with one general exception. Newsmen. The media were unabashedly and constantly interested in the corpsicle heirs, priority based on the money they stood to inherit. We faced a depressing hypothesis: the potential kidnappers were spending all their time watching the boob cube, letting the media do their tracking for them. But perhaps the connection was closer.

We started investigating newscast stations.

In mid-February I pulled Holden Chambers in and had him examined for an outlaw tracer. It was a move of desperation. Organleggers don't use such tools. They specialize in medicine. Our own tracer was still working, and it was the only tracer in him. Chambers was icily angry. We had interrupted his studying for a mid-term exam.

We managed to search three of the top dozen when they had medical checkups. Nothing.

Our investigations of the newscast stations turned up very little. Clark and Nash was running a good many one-time spots through NBA. Other advertising firms had similar lines of possible influence over other stations, broadcasting companies and cassette newszines. But we were looking for newsmen who had popped up from nowhere, with backgrounds forged or nonexistent. Ex-organleggers in new jobs. We didn't find any.

I called Menninger's one empty afternoon. Charlotte Chambers was still catatonic. "I've got Lowndes of New York working with me," Hartman told me. "He has precisely your voice, and good qualifications too. Charlotte hasn't responded yet. We've been wondering: could it have been the *way* you were talking?"

"You mean the accent? It's Kansas with an overlay of west coast and Belter."

"No, Lowndes has that too. I mean organlegger slang."

"I use it. Bad habit."

"That could be it." He made a face. "But we can't act on it. It might just scare her completely into herself."

"That's where she is now. I'd risk it."

"You're not a psychiatrist," he said.

I hung up and brooded. Negatives, all negatives.

I didn't hear the hissing sound until it was almost on me. I looked up then, and it was Luke Garner's ground-effect travel chair sliding accurately through the door. He watched me a moment, then said, "What are you looking so grim about?"

"Nothing. All the nothing we've been getting instead of results."

"Uh huh." He let the chair settle. "It's beginning to look like Tiller the Killer wasn't on assignment."

"That would blow the whole thing, wouldn't it? I did a lot of extrapolating from two beams of green light. One ex-organlegger tries to make holes in one ARM agent, and now we've committed tens of thousands of man-hours and seventy or eighty computer-hours on the strength of it. If they'd been planning to tie us up they couldn't have done it better."

"You know, I think you'd take it as a personal insult if Tiller shot at you just because he didn't like you."

I had to laugh. "How personal can you get?"

"That's better. Now will you stop sweating this? It's just another long shot. You know what legwork is like. We bet a lot of man-effort on this one because the odds looked good. Look how many organleggers would have to be in on it if it were true! We'd have a chance to snaffle them all. But if it doesn't work out, why sweat it?"

"The second Freezer Bill,'" I said, as if he didn't know.

"The Will of the People be done."

"Censor the people! They're murdering those dead men!"

Garner's face twitched oddly. I said, "What's funny?"

He let the laugh out. It sounded like a chicken screaming for help. "*Censor. Bleep.* They didn't used to be swear words. They were euphemisms. You'd put them in a book or on teevee, when you wanted a word they wouldn't let you use."

I shrugged. "Words are funny. *Damn* used to be a technical term in theology, if you want to look at it that way."

"I know, but they *sound* funny. When you start saying *bleep* and *censored* it ruins your masculine image."

"Censor my masculine image. What do we do about the corpsicle heirs? Call off the surveillance?"

"No. There's too much in the pot already." Garner looked broodingly into one bare wall of my office. "Wouldn't it be nice if we could persuade ten billion people to use prosthetics instead of transplants?"

Guilt glowed in my right arm, my left eye. I said, "Prosthetics don't feel. I might have settled for a prosthetic arm—" Dammit, I'd had the choice! "—but an eye? Luke, suppose it was possible to graft new legs on you. Would you take them?"

"Oh, dear, I do wish you hadn't asked me that," he said venomously.

"Sorry. I withdraw the question."

He brooded. It was a lousy thing to ask a man. He was still stuck with it; he couldn't spit it out.

I asked, "Did you have any special reason for dropping in?"

Luke shook himself. "Yah. I got the impression you were taking all this as a personal defeat. I stopped down to cheer you up."

We laughed at each other. "Listen," he said, "there are worse things than the organ bank problem. When I was young—your age, my child—it was almost impossible to get anyone convicted of a capital crime. Life sentences weren't for life. Psychology and psychiatry, such as they were, were concerned with curing criminals, returning them to society. The United States Supreme Court almost voted the death penalty unconstitutional."

"Sounds wonderful. How did it work out?"

"We had an impressive reign of terror. A lot of people got killed. Meanwhile transplant techniques were getting better and better. Eventually Vermont made the organ banks the official means of execution. That idea spread very damn fast."

"Yah." I remembered history courses.

"Now we don't even *have* prisons. The organ banks are always short. As soon as the UN votes the death penalty for a crime, most people stop committing it. Naturally."

"So we get the death penalty for having children without a license, or cheating on income tax, or running too many red traffic lights. Luke, I've seen what it *does* to people to keep voting more and more death penalties. They lose their respect for life."

"But the other situation was just as bad, Gil. Don't forget it."

"So now we've got the death penalty for being poor."

"The Freezer Law? I won't defend it. Except that that's the penalty for being poor and *dead*."

"Should it be a capital crime?"

"No, but it's not too bright either. If a man expects to be brought back to life, he should be prepared to pay the medical fees. Now, hold it. I know a lot of the pauper group had trust funds set up. They were wiped out by depressions, bad investments. Why the hell do you think banks take interest for a loan? They're being paid for the *risk*. The risk that the loan won't be paid back."

"Did you vote for the Freezer Law?"

"No, of course not."

"I must be spoiling for a fight. I'm glad you dropped by, Luke."

"Don't mention it."

"I keep thinking the ten billion voters will eventually work their way down to me. Go ahead, grin. Who'd want *your* liver?"

Garner cackled. "Somebody could murder me for my skeleton. Not to put inside him. For a museum."

We left it at that.

The news broke a couple of days later. Several North American hospitals had been reviving corpsicles.

How they had kept the secret was a mystery. Those corpsicles who had survived the treatment—twenty-two of them, out of thirty-five attempts—had been clinically alive for some ten months, conscious for shorter periods.

For the next week it was all the news there was. Taffy and I watched interviews with the dead men, with the doctors, with members of the Security Council. The move was not illegal. As publicity against the second Freezer Bill, it may have been a mistake.

All of the revived corpsicles had been insane. Else why risk it?

Some of the casualties had died because their insanity was caused by brain damage. The rest were—cured, but only in a biochemical sense. Each had been insane long enough for their doctors to decide that there was no hope. Now they were stranded in a foreign land, their homes forever lost in the mists of time. Revivification had saved them from an ugly, humiliating death at the hands of most of the human race, a fate that smacked of cannibalism and ghouls. The paranoids were hardly surprised. The rest reacted like paranoids.

In the boob cube they came across as a bunch of frightened mental patients.

One night we watched a string of interviews in the big screen in Taffy's bedroom wall. They weren't well handled. Too much 'How do you feel about the wonders of the present?' when the poor boobs hadn't come out of their shells long enough to know or care. Many wouldn't believe anything they were told or shown. Others didn't care about anything but space exploration—a largely Belter activity which Earth's voting public tended to ignore. Too much of it was at the level of this last one: an interviewer explaining to a woman that a boob cube was not a *cube,* that the word referred only to the three-dimensional effect. The poor woman was badly rattled and not too bright in the first place.

Taffy was sitting cross-legged on the bed, combing out her long, dark hair so that it flowed over her shoulders in shining curves. "She's an early one," she said critically. "There may have been oxygen starvation of the brain during freezing."

"That's what *you* see. All the average citizen sees is the way she acts. She's obviously not ready to join society."

"Dammit, Gil, she's *alive*. Shouldn't that be miracle enough for anyone?"

"Maybe. Maybe the average voter liked her better the other way."

Taffy brushed at her hair with angry vigor. "They're *alive*."

"I wonder if they revived Leviticus Hale."

"Leviti—? Oh. Not at Saint John's." Taffy worked there. She'd know.

"I haven't seen him in the cube. They should have revived him," I said. "With that patriarchal visage he'd make a *great* impression. He might even try the Messiah bit. 'Yea, brethren, I have returned from the dead to lead you—' None of the others have tried that yet."

"Good thing, too." Her strokes slowed. "A lot of them died in the thawing process, and afterward. From cell wall ruptures."

Ten minutes later I got up and used the phone. Taffy showed her amusement. "Is it that important?"

"Maybe not." I dialed the Vault of Eternity in New Jersey. I knew I'd be wondering until I did.

Mr. Restarick was on night watch. He seemed glad to see me. He'd have been glad to see anyone who would talk back. His clothes were the same mismatch of ancient styles, but they didn't look as anachronistic now. The boob cube had been infested with corpsicles wearing approximations of their own styles.

Yes, he remembered me. Yes, Leviticus Hale was still in place. The hospitals had taken two of his wards, and both had survived, he told me proudly. The administrators had wanted Hale too; they'd liked his looks and his publicity value, dating as he did from the last century but one. But they hadn't been able to get permission from the next of kin.

Taffy watched me watching a blank phone screen. "What's wrong?"

"The Chambers kid. Remember Holden Chambers, the corpsicle heir? He lied to me. He refused permission for the hospitals to revive Leviticus Hale. A *year* ago."

"Oh." She thought it over, then reacted with a charity

typical of her. "It's a lot of money just for not signing a paper."

The cube was showing an old flick, a remake of a Shakespeare play. We turned it to landscape and went to sleep.

I back away, back away. The composite ghost comes near, using somebody's arm and somebody's eye and Loren's pleural cavity containing somebody's heart and somebody's lung and somebody's other lung and I can feel it all inside him. Horrible. I reach deeper. Somebody's heart leaps like a fish in my hand.

Taffy found me in the kitchen making hot chocolate. For two. I know damn well she can't sleep when I'm restless. She said, "Why don't you tell me about it?"

"Because it's ugly."

"I think you'd better tell me." She came into my arms, rubbed her cheek against mine.

I said to her ear, "Get the poison out of my system? Sure, and into yours."

"All right." I could take it either way.

The chocolate was ready. I disengaged myself and poured it, added meager splashes of bourbon. She sipped reflectively. She said, "Is it always Loren?"

"Yah. Damn him."

"Never—this one you're after now."

"Anubis? I never dealt with him. He was Bera's assignment. Anyway, he retired before I was properly trained. Gave his territory to Loren. The market in stuff was so bad that Loren had to double his territory just to keep going." I was talking too much. I was desperate to talk to someone, to get back my grip on reality.

"What did they do, flip a coin?"

"For what? Oh. No, there was never a question about who was going to retire. Loren was a sick man. It must have been why he went into the business. He needed the supply of transplants. And he couldn't get out because he needed constant shots. His rejection spectrum must have been a bad joke. Anubis was different."

She sipped at her chocolate. She shouldn't have to know this, but I couldn't stop talking. "Anubis changed body parts at whim. We'll never get him. He probably made himself over completely when he . . . retired."

Taffy touched my shoulder. "Let's go back to bed."

"All right." But my own voice ran on in my head. *His only problem was the money. How could he hide a fortune that size? And the new identity. A new personality with lots of conspicuous money . . . and, if he tried to live somewhere else, a foreign accent too. But there's less privacy here, and he's known . . .* I sipped the chocolate, watching the landscape in the boob cube. *What could he do to make a new identity convincing?* The landscape scene was night on some mountaintop, bare tumbled rock backed by churning clouds. Restful.

I thought of something he could do.

I got out of bed and called Bera.

Taffy watched me in amazement. "It's three in the morning," she pointed out.

"I know."

Lila Bera was sleepy and naked and ready to kill someone. Me. She said, "Gil, it better be good."

"It's good. Tell Jackson I can locate Anubis."

Bera popped up beside her, demanded, "Where?" His hair was miraculously intact, a puffy black dandelion ready to blow. He was squint-eyed and grimacing with sleep, and as naked as . . . as I was, come to that. This thing superseded good manners.

I told him where Anubis was.

I had his attention then. I talked fast, sketching in the intermediate steps. "Does it sound reasonable? I can't tell. It's three in the morning. I may not be thinking straight."

Bera ran both hands through his hair, a swift, violent gesture that left his natural in shreds. "Why didn't I think of that? Why didn't *anyone* think of that?"

"The waste. When the stuff from one condemned ax murderer can save a dozen lives, it just doesn't occur to you—"

"Right right right. Skip that. What do we do?"

"Alert Headquarters. Then call Holden Chambers. I may be able to tell just by talking to him. Otherwise we'll have to go over."

"Yah." Bera grinned through the pain of interrupted sleep. "He's not going to like being called at three in the morning."

The white-haired man informed me that Holden Chambers was not to be disturbed. He was reaching for a (mythical) cutoff switch when I said, "ARM business, life and death," and displayed my ARM ident. He nodded and put me on hold.

Very convincing. But he'd gone through some of the same motions every time I'd called.

Chambers appeared, wearing a badly wrinkled cloth sleeping jacket. He backed up a few feet (wary of ghostly intrusions?) and sat down on the uneasy edge of a water bed. He rubbed his eyes and said, "Censor it, I was up past midnight studying. What now?"

"You're in danger. Immediate danger. Don't panic, but don't go back to bed either. We're coming over."

"You're kidding." He studied my face in the phone screen. "You're not, are you? A-a-all right, I'll put some clothes on. What kind of danger?"

"I can't tell you that. Don't go anywhere."

I called Bera back.

He met me in the lobby. We used his taxi. An ARM ident in the credit slot turns any cab into a police car. Bera said, "Couldn't you tell?"

"No, he was too far back. I had to say *something,* so I warned him not to go anywhere."

"I wonder if that was a good idea."

"It doesn't matter. Anubis only has about fifteen minutes to act, and even then we could follow him."

There was no immediate answer to our ring. Maybe he was surprised to see us outside his door. Ordinarily you can't get into the parking roof elevator unless a tenant lets you in; but an ARM ident unlocks most locks.

Bera's patience snapped. "I think he's gone. We'd better call—"

Chambers opened the door. "All right, what's it all about? Come—" He saw our guns.

Bera hit the door hard and branched right; I branched left. Those tiny apartments don't have many places to hide. The water bed was gone, replaced by an L-shaped couch and coffee table. There was nothing behind the couch. I covered the bathroom while Bera kicked the door open.

Nobody here but us. Chambers lost his astonished look, smiled and clapped for us. I bowed.

"You *must* have been serious," he said. "What kind of danger? Couldn't it have waited for morning?"

"Yah, but I couldn't have slept," I said, coming toward him. "I'm going to owe you a big fat apology if this doesn't work out."

He backed away.

"Hold still. This will only take a second." I advanced on him. Bera was behind him now. He hadn't hurried. His long legs give him deceptive speed.

Chambers backed away, backed away, backed into Bera and squeaked in surprise. He dithered, then made a break for the bathroom.

Bera reached out, wrapped one arm around Chambers' waist and pinned his arms with the other. Chambers struggled like a madman. I stepped wide around them, moved in sideways to avoid Chambers' thrashing legs, reached out to touch his face with my imaginary hand.

He froze. Then he screamed.

"That's what you were afraid of," I told him. "You never dreamed I could reach through a phone screen to do *this*." I reached into his head, felt smooth muscle and grainy bone and sinus cavities like bubbles. He tossed his head, but my hand went with it. I ran imaginary fingertips along the smooth inner surface of his skull. It was there. A ridge of scar, barely raised above the rest of the bone, too fine for X-rays. It ran in a closed curve from the base of his skull up through the temples to intersect his eye sockets.

"It's him," I said.

Bera screamed in his ear. "You *pig!*"

Anubis went limp.

"I can't find a joining at the brain stem. They must have transplanted the spinal cord too: the whole central nervous system." I found scars along the vertebrae. "That's what they did, all right."

Anubis spoke almost casually, as if he'd lost a chess game. "All right, that's a gotcha. I concede. Let's sit down."

"Sure." Bera threw him at the couch. He hit it, more

or less. He adjusted himself, looking astonished at Bera's bad behavior. What was the man so excited about?

Bera told him. "You pig. Coring him like that, making a vehicle out of the poor bastard. We never thought of a brain transplant."

"It's a wonder I thought of it myself. The stuff from one donor is worth over a million marks in surgery charges. Why should anyone use a whole donor for one transplant? But once I thought of it, it made all kinds of sense. The stuff wasn't selling anyway."

Funny: they both talked as if they'd known each other a long time. There aren't many people an organlegger will regard as *people*, but an ARM is one of them. We're organleggers too, in a sense.

Bera was holding a sonic on him. Anubis ignored it. He said, "The only problem was the money."

"Then you thought of the corpsicle heirs," I said.

"Yah. I went looking for a rich corpsicle with a young, healthy direct-line heir. Leviticus Hale seemed made for the part. He was the first one I noticed."

"He's pretty noticeable, isn't he? A healthy middle-aged man sleeping there among all those battered accident cases. Only two heirs, both orphans, one kind of introverted, the other . . . What did you do to Charlotte?"

"Charlotte Chambers? We drove her mad. We had to. She was the only one who'd notice if Holden Chambers suddenly got too different."

"What did you *do* to her?"

"We made a wirehead out of her."

"The hell. Someone would have noticed the contact in her scalp."

"No, no, no. We used one of those helmets you find in the ecstasy shops. It stimulates a current in the pleasure center of the brain, by induction, so a customer can try it out before the peddler actually drops the wire into his brain. We kept her in the helmet for nine days, on full. When we stopped the current, she just wasn't interested in anything any more."

"How did you know it would work?"

"Oh, we tried it out on a few prospects. It worked fine. It didn't hurt them after they were broken up."

"Okay." I went to the phone and dialed ARM Headquarters.

"It solved the money problem beautifully," he ran on. "I plowed most of it into advertising charges. And there's nothing suspicious about Leviticus Hale's money. When the second Freezer Bill goes through—well, I guess not. Not now. Unless—"

"No," Bera said for both of us.

I told the man on duty where we were, and to stop monitoring the tracers, and to call in the operatives watching corpsicle heirs. Then I hung up.

"I spent six months studying Chambers' college courses. I didn't want to blow his career. Six months! Answer me one," said Anubis, curiously anxious. "Where did I go wrong? What gave me away?"

"You were beautiful," I told him wearily. "You never went out of character. You should have been an actor. Would have been safer, too. We didn't suspect anything until—" I looked at my watch. "Forty-five minutes ago."

"Censored dammit! You would say that. When I saw you looking at me in Midgard I thought that was it. That floating cigarette. You'd got Loren, now you were after me."

I couldn't help it. I roared. Anubis sat there, taking it. He was beginning to blush.

They were shouting something, something I couldn't make out. Something with a beat. *DAdadada-DAdadada . . .*

There was just room for me and Jackson Bera and Luke Garner's travel chair on the tiny balcony outside Garner's office. Far below, the marchers flowed past the ARM building in half orderly procession. Teams of them carried huge banners. LET THEM STAY DEAD, one suggested, and another in small print: *why not revive them a bit at a time?* FOR YOUR FATHER'S SAKE, a third said with deadly logic.

They were roped off from the spectators, roped off into a column down the middle of Wilshire. The spectators were even thicker. It looked like all of Los Angeles had turned out to watch. Some of them carried placards

too. THEY WANT TO LIVE TOO, and ARE YOU A FREEZER
VAULT HEIR?

"What is it they're shouting?" Bera wondered. "It's
not the marchers, it's the spectators. They're drowning
out the marchers."

DAdadadaDAdadadaDAdadada, it rippled up to us
on stray wind currents.

"We could see it better inside, in the boob cube,"
Garner said without moving. What held us was a meta-
physical force, the knowledge that one is *there,* a wit-
ness.

Abruptly Garner asked, "How's Charlotte Chambers?"

"I don't know." I didn't want to talk about it.

"Didn't you call Menninger Institute this morning?"

"I mean I don't know how to take it. They've done a
wirehead operation on her. They're giving her just
enough current to keep her interested. It's *working,* I
mean she's *talking* to people, but . . ."

"It's got to be better than being catatonic," Bera said.

"Does it? There's no way to turn off a wirehead.
She'll have to go through life with a battery under her
hat. When she comes back far enough into the real
world, she'll find a way to boost the current and bug
right out again."

"Think of her as walking wounded." Bera shrugged,
shifting an invisible weight on his shoulders. "There *isn't*
any good answer. She's been *hurt,* man!"

"There's more to it than that," said Luke Garner.
"We need to know if she can be cured. There are more
wireheads every day. It's a new vice. We need to learn
how to control it. What the bleep is happening down
there?"

The bystanders were surging against the ropes. Suddenly they were through in a dozen places, coverging on
the marchers. It was a swirling mob scene. They were
still chanting, and suddenly I caught it.

ORganleggersORganleggersORganleggers . . .

"That's it!" Bera shouted in pleased surprise. "Anubis is getting too much publicity. It's good versus evil!"

The rioters started to collapse in curved ribbon patterns. Copters overhead were spraying them with sonic
stun cannon.

Bera said, "They'll never pass the second Freezer Bill now."

Never is a long time to Luke Garner. He said, "Not this time, anyway. We ought to start thinking about that. A lot of people have been applying for operations. There's quite a waiting list. When the second Freezer Bill fails—"

I saw it. "They'll start going to organleggers. We can keep track of them. Tracers."

"That's what I had in mind."

ARM

The ARM building had been abnormally quiet for some months now.

We'd needed the rest—at first. But these last few mornings the silence had had an edgy quality. We waved at each other on our paths to our respective desks, but our heads were elsewhere. Some of us had a restless look. Others were visibly, determinedly busy.

Nobody wanted to join a mother hunt.

This past year we'd managed to cut deep into the organlegging activities in the West Coast area. Pats on the back all around, but the results were predictable: other activities were going to increase. Sooner or later the newstapers would start screaming about stricter enforcement of the Fertility Laws, and then we'd all be out hunting down illegitimate parents . . . all of us who were not involved in something else.

It was high time I got involved in something else.

This morning I walked to my office through the usual edgy silence. I ran coffee from the spigot, carried it to my desk, punched for messages at the computer terminal. A slender file slid from the slot. A hopeful sign. I picked it up—one-handed, so that I could sip coffee as I went through it—and let it fall open in the middle.

Color holographs jumped out at me. I was looking down through a pair of windows over two morgue tables.

Stomach to brain: LURCH! What a hell of an hour to be looking at people with their faces burnt off! Get eyes to look somewhere else, and don't try to swallow that coffee. Why don't you change jobs?

They were hideous. Two of them, a man and a wom-

116

an. Something had burnt their faces away down to the skulls and beyond: bones and teeth charred, brain tissue cooked.

I swallowed and kept looking. I'd seen the dead before. These had just hit me at the wrong time.

Not a laser weapon, I thought . . . though that was chancy. There are thousands of jobs for lasers, and thousands of varieties to do the jobs. Not a hand laser, anyway. The pencil-thin beam of a hand laser would have chewed channels in the flesh. This had been a wide, steady beam of some kind.

I flipped back to the beginning and skimmed.

Details: They'd been found on the Wilshire slidewalk in West Los Angeles around 4:30 A.M. People don't use the slidewalks that late. They're afraid of organleggers. The bodies could have traveled up to a couple of miles before anyone saw them.

Preliminary autopsy: They'd been dead three or four days. No signs of drugs or poisons or puncture marks. Apparently the burns had been the only cause of death.

It must have been quick, then: a single flash of energy. Otherwise they'd have tried to dodge, and there'd be burns elsewhere. There were none. Just the faces, and char marks around the collars.

There was a memo from Bates, the coroner. From the looks of them, they might have been killed by some new weapon. So he'd sent the file over to us. Could we find anything in the ARM files that would fire a blast of heat or light a foot across?

I sat back and stared into the holos and thought about it.

A light weapon with a beam a foot across? They make lasers in that size, but as war weapons, used from orbit. One of those would have vaporized the heads, not charred them.

There were other possibilities. Death by torture, with the heads held in clamps in the blast from a commercial attitude jet. Or some kind of weird industrial accident: a flash explosion that had caught them both looking over a desk or something. Or even a laser beam reflected from a convex mirror.

Forget about its being an accident. The way the bodies were abandoned reeked of guilt, of something to be covered up. Maybe Bates was right. A new, illegal weapon.

And I could be deeply involved in searching for it when the mother hunt started.

The ARM has three basic functions. We hunt organleggers. We monitor world technology: new developments that might create new weapons, or that might affect the world economy or the balance of power among nations. And we enforce the Fertility Laws.

Come, let us be honest with ourselves. Of the three, protecting the Fertility Laws is probably the most important.

Organleggers don't aggravate the population problem.

Monitoring of technology is necessary enough, but it may have happened too late. There are enough fusion power plants and fusion rocket motors and fusion crematoria and fusion seawater distilleries around to let any madman or group thereof blow up the Earth or any selected part of it.

But if a lot of people in one region started having illegal babies, the rest of the world would scream. Some nations might even get mad enough to abandon population control. Then what? We've got eighteen billion on Earth now. We couldn't handle more.

So the mother hunts are necessary. But I hate them. It's no fun hunting down some poor sick woman so desperate to have children that she'll go through hell to avoid her six-month contraceptive shots. I'll get out of it if I can.

I did some obvious things. I sent a note to Bates at the coroner's office. *Send all further details on the autopsies, and let me know if the corpses are identified.* Retinal prints and brain-wave patterns were obviously out, but they might get something on gene patterns and fingerprints.

I spent some time wondering where two bodies had been kept for three to four days, and why, before being abandoned in a way that could have been used three days earlier. But that was a problem for the LAPD detectives. Our concern was with the weapon.

So I started writing a search pattern for the computer: find me a widget that will fire a beam of a given description. From the pattern of penetration into skin and bone and brain tissue, there was probably a way to express the frequency of the light as a function of the duration of the blast, but I didn't fool with that. I'd pay for my laziness later, when the computer handed me a foot-thick list of light-emitting machinery and I had to wade through it.

I had punched in the instructions, and was relaxing with more coffee and a cigarette, when Ordaz called.

Detective-Inspector Julio Ordaz was a slender, dark-skinned man with straight black hair and soft black eyes. The first time I saw him in a phone screen, he had been telling me of a good friend's murder. Two years later I still flinched when I saw him.

"Hello, Julio. Business or pleasure?"

"Business, Gil. It is to be regretted."

"Yours or mine?"

"Both. There is murder involved, but there is also a machine . . . Look, can you see it behind me?" Ordaz stepped out of the field of view, then reached invisibly to turn the phone camera.

I looked into somebody's living room. There was a wide circle of discoloration in the green indoor grass rug. In the center of the circle, a machine and a man's body.

Was Julio putting me on? The body was old, half mummified. The machine was big and cryptic in shape, and it glowed with a subdued, eery blue light.

Ordaz sounded serious enough. "Have you ever seen anything like this?"

"No. That's some machine." Unmistakably an experimental device: no neat plastic case, no compactness, no assembly-line welding. Too complex to examine through a phone camera, I decided. "Yah, that looks like something for us. Can you send it over?"

Ordaz came back on. He was smiling, barely. "I'm afraid we cannot do that. Perhaps you should send someone here to look at it."

"Where are you now?"

"In Raymond Sinclair's apartment on the top floor of the Rodewald Building in Santa Monica."

"I'll come myself," I said. My tongue suddenly felt thick.

"Please land on the roof. We are holding the elevator for examination."

"Sure." I hung up.

Raymond Sinclair!

I'd never met Raymond Sinclair. He was something of a recluse. But the ARM had dealt with him once, in connection with one of his inventions, the FyreStop device. And everyone knew that he had lately been working on an interstellar drive. It was only a rumor, of course . . . but if someone had killed the brain that held that secret . . .

I went.

The Rodewald Building was forty stories of triangular prism with a row of triangular balconies going up each side. The balconies stopped at the thirty-eighth floor.

The roof was a garden. There were rose bushes in bloom along one edge, full-grown elms nestled in ivy along another, and a miniature forest of Bonsai trees along the third. The landing pad and carport were in the center. A squad car was floating down ahead of my taxi. It landed, then slid under the carport to give me room to land.

A cop in vivid orange uniform came out to watch me come down. I couldn't tell what he was carrying until I had stepped out. It was a deep-sea fishing pole, still in its kit.

He said, "May I see some ID, please?"

I had my ARM ident in my hand. He checked it in the console in the squad car, then handed it back. "The Inspector's waiting downstairs," he said.

"What's the pole for?"

He smiled suddenly, almost secretively. "You'll see."

We left the garden smells via a flight of concrete stairs. They led down into a small room half full of gardening tools, and a heavy door with a spy-eye in it. Ordaz opened the door for us. He shook my hand briskly, glanced at the cop. "You found something? Good."

The cop said, "There's a sporting goods store six blocks from here. The manager let me borrow it. He made sure I knew the name of the store."

"Yes, there will certainly be publicity on this matter.

Come, Gil—" Ordaz took my arm. "You should examine this before we turn it off."

No garden smells here, but there was something—a whiff of something long dead, that the air conditioning hadn't quite cleared away. Ordaz walked me into the living room.

It looked like somebody's idea of a practical joke.

The indoor grass covered Sinclair's living room floor, wall to wall. In a perfect fourteen-foot circle between the sofa and the fireplace, the rug was brown and dead. Elsewhere it was green and thriving.

A man's mummy, dressed in stained slacks and turtleneck, lay on its back in the center of the circle. At a guess it had been about six months dead. It wore a big wristwatch with extra dials on the face and a fine-mesh platinum band, loose now around a wrist of bones and brown skin. The back of the skull had been smashed open, possibly by the classic blunt instrument lying next to it.

If the fireplace was false—it almost had to be; nobody burns wood—the fireplace instruments were genuine nineteenth or twentieth century antiques. The rack was missing a poker. A poker lay inside the circle, in the dead grass next to the disintegrating mummy.

The glowing goldberg device sat just in the center of the magic circle.

I stepped forward, and a man's voice spoke sharply. "Don't go inside that circle of rug. It's more dangerous than it looks."

It was a man I knew: Officer-One Valpredo, a tall man with a small, straight mouth and a long, narrow Italian face.

"Looks dangerous enough to me," I said.

"It is. I reached in there myself," Valpredo told me, "right after we got here. I thought I could flip the switch off. My whole arm went numb. Instantly. No feeling at all. I yanked it away fast, but for a minute or so after that my whole arm was dead meat. I thought I'd lost it. Then it was all pins and needles, like I'd slept on it."

The cop who had brought me in had almost finished assembling the deep-sea fishing pole.

Ordaz waved into the circle. "Well? Have you ever seen anything like this?"

I shook my head, studying the violet-glowing machinery. "Whatever it is, it's brand new. Sinclair's really done it this time."

An uneven line of solenoids was attached to a plastic frame with homemade joins. Blistered spots on the plastic showed where other objects had been attached and later removed. A breadboard bore masses of heavy wiring. There were six big batteries hooked in parallel, and a strange, heavy piece of sculpture in what we later discovered was pure silver, with wiring attached at three curving points. The silver was tarnished almost black and there were old file marks at the edges.

Near the center of the arrangement, just in front of the silver sculpture, were two concentric solenoids embedded in a block of clear plastic. They glowed blue shading to violet. So did the batteries. A less perceptible violet glow radiated from everywhere on the machine, more intensely in the interior parts.

That glow bothered me more than anything else. It was too theatrical. It was like something a special effects man might add to a cheap late-night thriller, to suggest a mad scientist's laboratory.

I moved around to get a closer look at the dead man's watch.

"Keep your head out of the field!" Valpredo said sharply.

I nodded. I squatted on my heels outside the borderline of dead grass.

The dead man's watch was going like crazy. The minute hand was circling the dial every seven seconds or so. I couldn't find the second hand at all.

I backed away from the arc of dead grass and stood up. Interstellar drive, hell. This blue-glowing monstrosity looked more like a time machine gone wrong.

I studied the single-throw switch welded to the plastic frame next to the batteries. A length of nylon line dangled from the horizontal handle. It looked like someone had tugged the switch *on* from outside the field by using the line; but he'd have had to hang from the ceiling to tug it *off* that way.

"I see why you couldn't send it over to ARM Headquarters. You can't even touch it. You stick your arm or your head in there for a second, and that's ten minutes without a blood supply."

Ordaz said, "Exactly."

"It looks like you could reach in there with a stick and flip that switch off."

"Perhaps. We are about to try that." He waved at the man with the fishing pole. "There was nothing in this room long enough to reach the switch. We had to send—"

"Wait a minute. There's a problem."

He looked at me. So did the cop with the fishing pole.

"That switch could be a self-destruct. Sinclair was supposed to be a secretive bastard. Or the—field might hold considerable potential energy. Something might go blooey."

Ordaz sighed. "We must risk it. Gil, we have measured the rotation of the dead man's wristwatch. One hour per seven seconds. Fingerprints, footprints, laundry marks, residual body odor, stray eyelashes, all disappearing at an hour per seven seconds." He gestured, and the cop moved in and began trying to hook the switch.

"Already we may never know just when he was killed," said Ordaz.

The tip of the pole wobbled in large circles, steadied beneath the switch, made contact. I held my breath. The pole bowed. The switch snapped up, and suddenly the violet glow was gone. Valpredo reached into the field, warily, as if the air might be red hot. Nothing happened, and he relaxed.

Then Ordaz began giving orders, and quite a lot happened. Two men in lab coats drew a chalk outline around the mummy and the poker. They moved the mummy onto a stretcher, put the poker in a plastic bag and put it next to the mummy.

I said, "Have you identified that?"

"I'm afraid so," said Ordaz. "Raymond Sinclair had his own autodoc—"

"*Did* he. Those things are expensive."

"Yes. Raymond Sinclair was a wealthy man. He owned the top two floors of this building, and the roof. According to records in his 'doc, he had a new set of bud teeth implanted two months ago." Ordaz pointed to the mummy, to the skinned-back dry lips and the buds of new teeth that were just coming in.

Right. That was Sinclair.

That brain had made miracles, and someone had smashed it with a wrought-iron rod. The interstellar drive . . . that glowing goldberg device? Or had it been still inside his head?

I said, "We'll have to get whoever did it. We'll *have* to. Even so . . ." Even so. No more miracles.

"We may have her already," Julio said.

I looked at him.

"There is a girl in the autodoc. We think she is Dr. Sinclair's great-niece, Janice Sinclair."

It was a standard drugstore autodoc, a thing like a giant coffin with walls a foot thick and a headboard covered with dials and red and green lights. The girl lay face up, her face calm, her breathing shallow. Sleeping Beauty. Her arms were in the guts of the 'doc, hidden by bulky rubbery sleeves.

She was lovely enough to stop my breath. Soft brown hair showing around the electrode cap; small, perfect nose and mouth; smooth pale blue skin shot with silver threads . . .

That last was an evening dye job. Without it the impact of her would have been much lessened. The blue shade varied slightly to emphasize the shape of her body and the curve of her cheekbones. The silver lines varied too, being denser in certain areas, guiding the eye in certain directions: to the tips of her breasts, or across the slight swell of abdominal muscle to a lovely oval navel.

She'd paid high for that dye job. But she would be beautiful without it.

Some of the headboard lights were red. I punched for a readout, and was jolted. The 'doc had been forced to amputate her right arm. Gangrene.

She was in for a hell of a shock when she woke up.

"All right," I said. "She's lost her arm. That doesn't make her a killer."

Ordaz asked, "If she were homely, would it help?"

I laughed. "You question my dispassionate judgment? Men have died for less!" Even so, I thought he could be right. There was good reason to think that the killer was now missing an arm.

"What do you think happened here, Gil?"

"Well . . . any way you look at it, the killer had to want to take Sinclair's, ah, time machine with him. It's priceless, for one thing. For another, it looks like he tried to set it up as an alibi. Which means that he knew about it before he came here." I'd been thinking this through. "Say he made sure some people knew where he was a few hours before he got here. He killed Sinclair within range of the . . . call it a generator. Turned it on. He figured Sinclair's own watch would tell him how much time he was gaining. Afterward he could set the watch back and leave with the generator. There'd be no way the police could tell he wasn't killed six hours earlier, or any number you like."

"Yes. But he did not do that."

"There was that line hanging from the switch. He must have turned it on from outside the field . . . probably because he didn't want to sit with the body for six hours. If he tried to step outside the field after he'd turned it on, he'd bump his nose. It'd be like trying to walk through a wall, going from field time to normal time. So he turned it off, stepped out of range and used that nylon line to turn it on again. He probably made the same mistake Valpredo did: he thought he could step back in and turn it off."

Ordaz nodded in satisfaction. "Exactly. It was very important for him—or her—to do that. Otherwise he would have no alibi and no profit. If he continued to try to reach into the field—"

"Yah, he could lose the arm to gangrene. That'd be convenient for us, wouldn't it? He'd be easy to find. But, look, Julio: the girl could have done the same thing to herself trying to *help* Sinclair. He might not have been that obviously dead when she got home."

"He might even have been alive," Ordaz pointed out. I shrugged.

"In point of fact, she came home at one ten, in her own car, which is still in the carport. There are cameras mounted to cover the landing pad and carport. Doctor Sinclair's security was thorough. This girl was the only arrival last night. There were no departures."

"From the roof, you mean."

"Gil, there are only two ways to leave these apartments. One is from the roof, and the other is by elevator, from the lobby. The elevator is on this floor, and it was turned off. It was that way when we arrived. There is no way to override that control from elsewhere in this building."

"So someone could have taken it up here and turned it off afterward . . . or Sinclair could have turned it off before he was killed . . . I see what you mean. Either way, the killer has to be still here." I thought about that. I didn't like its taste. "No, it doesn't fit. How could she be bright enough to work out that alibi, then dumb enough to lock herself in with the body?"

Ordaz shrugged. "She locked the elevator before killing her uncle. She did not want to be interrupted. Surely that was sensible? After she hurt her arm she must have been in a great hurry to reach the 'doc."

One of the red lights turned green. I was glad for that. She didn't look like a killer. I said, half to myself, "Nobody looks like a killer when he's asleep."

"No. But she is where a killer ought to be. *Qué lástima.*"

We went back to the living room. I called ARM Headquarters and had them send a truck.

The machine hadn't been touched. While we waited I borrowed a camera from Valpredo and took pictures of the setup *in situ*. Relative positions of the components might be important.

The lab men were in the brown grass using aerosol sprays to turn fingerprints white and give a vivid yellow glow to faint traces of blood. They got plenty of fingerprints on the machine, none at all on the poker. There was a puddle of yellow in the grass where the mummy's head had been, and a long yellow snail track ending at the business end of the poker. It looked like someone had tried to drag the poker out of the field after it had fallen.

Sinclair's apartments were roomy and comfortable and occupied the entire top floor. The lower floor was the laboratory where Sinclair had produced his miracles. I went through it with Valpredo. It wasn't that impressive. It looked like an expensive hobby setup. These tools would assemble components already fabricated, but they would not build anything complex.

—Except for the computer terminal. That was like a little womb, with a recline chair inside a three-hundred-and-sixty-degree wraparound holovision screen and enough banked controls to fly the damn thing to Alpha Centauris.

The secrets there must be in that computer! But I didn't try to use it. We'd have to send an ARM programmer to break whatever failsafe codes Sinclair had put in the memory banks.

The truck arrived. We dragged Sinclair's legacy up the stairs to the roof in one piece. The parts were sturdily mounted on their frame, and the stairs were wide and not too steep.

I rode home in the back of the truck. Studying the generator. That massive piece of silver had something of the look of *Bird In Flight*: a triangle operated on by a topology student, with wires at what were still the corners. I wondered if it was the heart of the machine, or just a piece of misdirection. Was I really riding with an interstellar drive? Sinclair could have started that rumor himself, to cover whatever this was. Or . . . there was a law against his working two projects simultaneously.

I was looking forward to Bera's reaction.

Jackson Bera came upon us moving it through the halls of ARM Headquarters. He trailed along behind us. Nonchalant. We pulled the machine into the main laboratory and started checking it against the holos I'd taken, in case something had been jarred loose. Bera leaned against the door jamb, watching us, his eyes gradually losing interest until he seemed about to go to sleep.

I'd met him three years ago, when I returned from the asteroids and joined the ARM. He'd been twenty then, and two years an ARM; but his father and grandfather had both been ARMs. Much of my training had come from Bera. And as I learned to hunt men who hunt other men, I had watched what it was doing to him.

An ARM needs empathy. He needs the ability to piece together a picture of the mind of his prey. But Bera had too much empathy. I remember his reaction when Kenneth Graham killed himself: a single surge of current through the plug in his skull and down the wire to the pleasure center of his brain. Bera had been twitchy for weeks. And the Anubis case early last year. When we realized what the man had done, Bera had been close to killing him on the spot. I wouldn't have blamed him.

Last year Bera had had enough. He'd gone into the technical end of the business. His days of hunting organleggers were finished. He was now running the ARM laboratory.

He *had* to want to know what this oddball contraption was. I kept waiting for him to ask . . . and he watched, faintly smiling. Finally it dawned on me. He thought it was a pratical joke, something I'd cobbled together for his own discomfiture.

I said, "Bera—"

And he looked at me brightly and said, "Hey, man, what is it?"

"You ask the most embarrassing questions."

"Right, I can understand your feeling that way, but what *is* it? I love it, it's neat, but what is this that you have brought me?"

I told him all I knew, such as it was. When I finished he said, "It doesn't sound much like a new space drive."

"Oho, you heard that too, did you? No, it doesn't. Unless—" I'd been wondering since I first saw it. "Maybe it's supposed to accelerate a fusion explosion. You'd get greater efficiency in a fusion drive."

"Nope. They get better than ninety percent now, and that widget looks *heavy*." He reached to touch the bent silver triangle, gently, with long, tapering fingers. "Huh. Well, we'll dig out the answers."

"Good luck. I'm going back to Sinclair's place."

"Why? The action is here." Often enough he'd heard me talking wistfully of joining an interstellar colony. He must know how I'd feel about a better drive for the interstellar slowboats.

"It's like this," I said. "We've got the generator, but we don't know anything about it. We might wreck it. I'm going to have a whack at finding someone who knows something about Sinclair's generator."

"Meaning?"

"Whoever tried to steal it. Sinclair's killer."

"If you say so." But he looked dubious. He knew me

too well. He said, "I understand there's a mother hunt in the offing."

"Oh?"

He smiled. "Just a rumor. You guys are lucky. When my dad first joined, the business of the ARM was *mostly* mother hunts. The organleggers hadn't really got organized yet, and the Fertility Laws were new. If we hadn't enforced them nobody would have obeyed them at all."

"Sure, and people threw rocks at your father. Bera, those days are *gone*."

"They could come back. Having children is basic."

"Bera, I did not join the ARM to hunt unlicensed parents." I waved and left before he could answer. I could do without the call to duty from Bera, who had done with hunting men and mothers.

I'd had a good view of the Rodewald Building, dropping toward the roof this morning. I had a good view now from my commandeered taxi. This time I was looking for escape paths.

There were no balconies on Sinclair's floors, and the windows were flush to the side of the building. A cat burglar would have trouble with them. They didn't look like they'd open.

I tried to spot the cameras Ordaz had mentioned as the taxi dropped toward the roof. I couldn't find them. Maybe they were mounted in the elms.

Why was I bothering? I hadn't joined the ARM to chase mothers or machinery or common murders. I'd joined to pay for my arm. My new arm had reached the World Organ Bank Facility via a captured organlegger's cache. Some honest citizen had died unwillingly on a city slidewalk, and now his arm was part of me.

I'd joined the ARM to hunt organleggers.

The ARM doesn't deal in murder *per se*. The machine was out of my hands now. A murder investigation wouldn't keep me out of a mother hunt. And I'd never met the girl. I knew nothing of her, beyond the fact that she was where a killer ought to be.

Was it just that she was pretty?

Poor Janice. When she woke up . . . For a solid

month I'd wakened to that same stunning shock, the knowledge that my right arm was gone.

The taxi settled. Valpredo was waiting below.

I speculated . . . Cars weren't the only things that flew. But anyone flying one of those tricky ducted-fan fly-cycles over a city, where he could fall on a pedestrian, wouldn't have to worry about a murder charge. They'd feed him to the organ banks regardless. And anything that flew would have to have left traces anywhere but on the landing pad itself. It would crush a rose bush or a Bonsai tree or be flipped over by an elm.

The taxi took off in a whisper of air.

Valpredo was grinning at me. "The Thinker. What's on your mind?"

"I was wondering if the killer could have come down on the carport roof."

He turned to study the situation. "There are two cameras mounted on the edge of the roof. If his vehicle was light enough, sure, he could land there, and the cameras wouldn't spot him. Roof wouldn't hold a car, though. Anyway, nobody did it."

"How do you know?"

"I'll show you. By the way, we inspected the camera system. We're pretty sure the cameras weren't tampered with."

"And nobody came down from the roof last night except the girl?"

"Nobody. Nobody even landed here until seven this morning. Look here." We had reached the concrete stairs that led down into Sinclair's apartments. Valpredo pointed at a glint of light in the sloping ceiling, at heart level. "This is the only way down. The camera would get anyone coming in or out. It might not catch his face, but it'd show if someone had passed. It takes sixty frames a minute."

I went on down. A cop let me in.

Ordaz was on the phone. The screen showed a young man with a deep tan and shock showing through the tan. Ordaz waved at me, a shushing motion, and went on talking. "Then you'll be here in fifteen minutes? That will be a great help to us. Please land on the roof. We are still working on the elevator."

He hung up and turned to me. "That was Andrew

Porter, Janice Sinclair's lover. He tells us that he and Janice spent the evening at a party. She dropped him off at his home around one o'clock."

"Then she came straight home, if that's her in the 'doc."

"I think it must be. Mr. Porter says she was wearing a blue skin-dye job." Ordaz was frowning. "He put on a most convincing act, if it was that. I think he really was not expecting any kind of trouble. He was surprised that a stranger answered, shocked when he learned of Doctor Sinclair's death, and horrified when he learned that Janice had been hurt."

With the mummy and the generator removed, the murder scene had become an empty circle of brown grass marked with random streaks of yellow chemical and outlines of white chalk.

"We had some luck," said Ordaz. "Today's date is June 4, 2124. Dr. Sinclair was wearing a calendar watch. It registered January 17, 2125. If we switched the machine off at ten minutes to ten—which we did—and if it was registering an hour for every seven seconds that passed outside the field, then the field must have gone on around one o'clock last night, give or take a margin of error."

"Then if the girl didn't do it, she must have just missed the killer."

"Exactly."

"What about the elevator? Could it have been jiggered?"

"No. We took the workings apart. It was on this floor, and locked by hand. Nobody could have left by elevator . . ."

"Why did you trail off like that?"

Ordaz shrugged, embarrassed. "This peculiar machine really does bother me, Gil. I found myself thinking, suppose it can reverse time? Then the killer could have gone down in an elevator that was going up."

He laughed with me. I said, "In the first place, I don't believe a word of it. In the second place, he didn't have the machine to do it with. Unless . . . he made his escape before the murder. Dammit, now you've got me doing it."

"I would like to know more about the machine."

"Bera's investigating it now. I'll let you know as soon as we learn anything. And *I'd* like to know more about how the killer couldn't possibly have left."

He looked at me. "Details?"

"Could someone have opened a window?"

"No. These apartments are forty years old. The smog was still bad when they were built. Dr. Sinclair apparently preferred to depend on his air conditioning."

"How about the apartment below? I presume it has a different set of elevators—"

"Yes, of course. It belongs to Howard Rodewald, the owner of this building—of this chain of buildings, in fact. At the moment he is in Europe. His apartment has been loaned to friends."

"There's no stairs down to there?"

"No. We searched these apartments thoroughly."

"All right. We know the killer had a nylon line, because he left a strand of it on the generator. Could he have climbed down to Rodewald's balcony from the roof?"

"Thirty feet? Yes, I suppose so." Ordaz' eyes sparked. "We must look into that. There is still the matter of how he got past the camera, and whether he could have gotten inside once he was on the balcony."

"Yah."

"Try this, Gil. Another question. How did he *expect* to get away?" He watched for my reaction, which must have been satisfying, because it *was* a damn good question. "You see, if Janice Sinclair murdered her great-uncle, then neither question applies. If we are looking for someone else, we have to assume that his plans misfired. He had to improvise."

"Uh huh. He could still have been planning to use Rodewald's balcony. And that would mean he had a way past the camera . . ."

"Of course he did. The generator."

Right. If he came to steal the generator . . . and he'd have to steal it regardless, because if we found it here it would shoot his alibi sky high. So he'd leave it on while he trundled it up the stairs. Say it took him a minute; that's only an eighth of a second of normal time. One chance in eight that the camera would fire, and it would catch nothing but a streak . . . "Uh oh."

"What is it?"

"He had to be planning to steal the machine. Is he really going to lower it to Rodewald's balcony by *rope?*"

"I think it unlikely," said Ordaz. "It weighed more than fifty pounds. He could have moved it upstairs. The frame would make it portable. But to lower it by rope . . ."

"We'd be looking for one hell of an athlete."

"At least you will not have to search far to find him. We assume that your hypothetical killer came by elevator, do we not?"

"Yah." Nobody but Janice Sinclair had arrived by the roof last night.

"The elevator was programed to allow a number of people to enter it, and to turn away all others. The list is short. Doctor Sinclair was not a gregarious man."

"You're checking them out? Wherabouts, alibis and so forth?"

"Of course."

"There's something else you might check on," I said. But Andrew Porter came in and I had to postpone it.

Porter came casual, in a well worn translucent one-piece jump suit he must have pulled on while running for a taxi. The muscles rolled like boulders beneath the loose fabric, and his belly muscles showed like the plates on an armadillo. Surfing muscles. The sun had bleached his hair nearly white and burned him as brown as Jackson Bera. You'd think a tan that dark would cover for blood draining out of a face, but it doesn't.

"Where is she?" he demanded. He didn't wait for an answer. He knew where the 'doc was, and he went there. We trailed in his wake.

Ordaz didn't push. He waited while Porter looked down at Janice, then punched for a readout and went through it in detail. Porter seemed calmer then, and his color was back. He turned to Ordaz and said, "What happened?"

"Mr. Porter, did you know anything of Dr. Sinclair's latest project?"

"The time compressor thing? Yah. He had it set up in the living room when I got here yesterday evening—right in the middle of that circle of dead grass. Any connection?"

"When did you arrive?"

"Oh, about . . . six. We had some drinks, and Uncle Ray showed off his machine. He didn't tell us much about it. Just showed what it could do." Porter showed us flashing white teeth. "It *worked*. That thing can compress time! You could live your whole life in there in two months! Watching him move around inside the field was like trying to keep track of a hummingbird. Worse. He struck a match—"

"When did you leave?"

"About eight. We had dinner at Cziller's House of Irish Coffee, and— Listen, what *happened* here?"

"There are some things we need to know first, Mr. Porter. Were you and Janice together for all of last evening? Were there others with you?"

"Sure. We had dinner alone, but afterward we went to a kind of party. On the beach at Santa Monica. Friend of mine has a house there. I'll give you the address. Some of us wound up back at Cziller's around midnight. Then Janice flew me home."

"You have said that you are Janice's lover. Doesn't she live with you?"

"No. I'm her steady lover, you might say, but I don't have any strings on her." He seemed embarrassed. "She lives here with Uncle Ray. Lived. Oh, *hell*." He glanced into the 'doc. "Look, the readout said she'll be waking up any minute. Can I get her a robe?"

"Of course."

We followed Porter to Janice's bedroom, where he picked out a peach-colored negligée for her. I was beginning to like the guy. He had good instincts. An evening dye job was not the thing to wear on the morning of a murder. And he'd picked one with long, loose sleeves. Her missing arm wouldn't show so much.

"You call him Uncle Ray," said Ordaz.

"Yah. Because Janice did."

"He did not object? Was he gregarious?"

"Gregarious? Well, no, but *we* liked each other. We both liked puzzles, you understand? We traded murder mysteries and jigsaw puzzles. Listen, this may sound silly, but are you sure he's dead?"

"Regrettably, yes. He is dead, and murdered. Was he expecting someone to arrive after you left?"

"Yes."

"He said so?"

"No. But he was wearing a shirt and pants. When it was just us he usually went naked."

"Ah."

"Older people don't do that much," Porter said. "But Uncle Ray was in good shape. He took care of himself."

"Have you any idea whom he might have been expecting?"

"No. Not a woman; not a date, I mean. Maybe someone in the same business."

Behind him, Janice moaned.

Porter was hovering over her in a flash. He put a hand on her shoulder and urged her back. "Lie still, love. We'll have you out of there in a jiffy."

She waited while he disconnected the sleeves and other paraphernalia. She said, "What happened?"

"They haven't told me yet," Porter said with a flash of anger. "Be careful sitting up. You've had an accident."

"What kind of—? *Oh!*"

"It'll be all right."

"My *arm!*"

Porter helped her out of the 'doc. Her arm ended in pink flesh two inches below the shoulder. She let Porter drape the robe around her. She tried to fasten the sash, quit when she realized she was trying to do it with one hand.

I said, "Listen, I lost my arm once."

She looked at me. So did Porter.

"I'm Gil Hamilton. With the UN Police. You reallly don't have anything to worry about. See?" I raised my right arm, opened and closed the fingers. "The organ banks don't get much call for arms, as compared to kidneys, for instance. You probably won't even have to wait. I didn't. It feels just like the arm I was born with, and it works just as well."

"How did you lose it?" she asked.

"Ripped away by a meteor," I said, not without pride. "While I was asteroid mining in the Belt." I didn't have to tell her that we'd caused the meteor cluster ourselves, by setting the bomb wrong on an asteroid we wanted to move.

Ordaz said to her, "Do you remember how you lost your own arm?"

"Yes." She shivered. "Could we go somewhere where I could sit down? I feel a bit weak."

We moved to the living room. Janice dropped onto the couch a bit too hard. It might have been shock, or the missing arm might be throwing her balance off. I remembered. She said, "Uncle Ray's dead, isn't he?"

"Yes."

"I came home and found him that way. Lying next to that time machine of his, and the back of his head all bloody. I thought maybe he was still alive, but I could see the machine was going; it had that violet glow. I tried to get hold of the poker. I wanted to use it to switch the machine off, but I couldn't get a grip. My arm wasn't just numb, it wouldn't move. You know, you can try to wiggle your toes when your foot's asleep, but . . . I could get my hands on the handle of the damn poker, but when I tried to pull it just slid off."

"You kept trying?"

"For awhile. Then . . . I backed away to think it over. I wasn't about to waste any time, with Uncle Ray maybe dying in there. My arm felt stone dead . . . I guess it was, wasn't it?" She shuddered. "Rotting meat. It smelled that way. And all of a sudden I felt so weak and dizzy, like I was dying myself. I barely made it into the 'doc."

"Good thing you did," I said. The blood was leaving Porter's face again as he realized what a close thing it had been.

Ordaz said, "Was your great-uncle expecting visitors last night?"

"I think so."

"Why do you think so?"

"I don't know. He just—acted that way."

"We are told that you and some friends reached Cziller's House of Irish Coffee around midnight. Is that true?"

"I guess so. We had some drinks, then I took Drew home and came home myself."

"Straight home?"

"Yes." She shivered. "I put the car away and went downstairs. I knew something was wrong. The door was open. Then there was Uncle Ray lying next to that machine! I knew better than to just run up to him. He'd told us not to step into the field."

"Oh? Then you should have known better than to reach for the poker."

"Well, yes. I could have used the tongs," she said as if the idea had just occurred to her. "It's just as long. I didn't think of it. There wasn't *time*. Don't you understand, he was dying in there, or dead!"

"Yes, of course. Did you interfere with the murder scene in any way?"

She laughed bitterly. "I suppose I moved the poker about two inches. Then when I felt what was happening to me I just ran for the 'doc. It was awful. Like dying."

"Instant gangrene," said Porter.

Ordaz said, "You did not, for example, lock the elevator?"

Damn! I should have thought of that.

"No. We usually do, when we lock up for the night, but I didn't have time."

Porter said, "Why?"

"The elevator was locked when we arrived," Ordaz told him.

Porter ruminated that. "Then the killer must have left by the roof. You'll have pictures of him."

Ordaz smiled apologetically. "That is our problem. No cars left the roof last night. Only one car arrived. That was yours, Miss Sinclair."

"But," said Porter, and he stopped. He thought it through again. "Did the police turn on the elevator again after they got here?"

"No. The killer could not have left after we got here."

"Oh."

"What happened was this," said Ordaz. "Around five thirty this morning, the tenants in—" He stopped to remember. "In 36A called the building maintenance man about a smell as of rotting meat coming through the air conditioning system. He spent some time looking for the source, but once he reached the roof it was obvious. He—"

Porter pounced. "He reached the roof in what kind of vehicle?"

"Mr. Steeves says that he took a taxi from the street.

There is no other way to reach Dr. Sinclair's private landing pad, is there?"

"No. But why would he do that?"

"Perhaps there have been other times when strange smells came from Dr. Sinclair's laboratory. We will ask him."

"Do that."

"Mr. Steeves followed the smell through the doctor's open door. He called us. He waited for us on the roof."

"What about his taxi?" Porter was hot on the scent. "Maybe the killer just waited till that taxi got here, then took it somewhere else when Steeves finished with it."

"It left immediately Steeves had stepped out. He had a taxi clicker if he wanted another. The cameras were on it the entire time it was on the roof." Ordaz paused. "You see the problem?"

Apparently Porter did. He ran both hands through his white-blond hair. "I think we ought to put off discussing it until we know more."

He meant Janice. Janice looked puzzled; she hadn't caught on. But Ordaz nodded at once and stood up. "Very well. There is no reason Miss Sinclair cannot go on living here. We may have to bother you again," he told her. "For now, our condolences."

He made his exit. I trailed along. So, unexpectedly, did Drew Porter. At the top of the stairs he stopped Ordaz with a big hand around the Inspector's upper arm. "You're thinking Janice did it, aren't you?"

Ordaz sighed. "What choice have I? I must consider the possibility."

"She didn't have any reason. She loved Uncle Ray. She's lived with him on and off these past twelve years. She hasn't got the slighest reason to kill him."

"Is there no inheritance?"

His expression went sour. "All right, *yes*, she'll have some money coming. But Janice wouldn't care about anything like that!"

"Ye-es. Still, what choice have I? Everything we now know tells us that the killer could not have left the scene of the killing. We searched the premises immediately. There was only Janice Sinclair and her murdered uncle."

Porter bit back an answer, chewed it . . . He must

have been tempted. Amateur detective, one step ahead of the police all the way. Yes, Watson, these *gendarmes* have a talent for missing the obvious . . . But he had too much to lose. Porter said, "And the maintenance man. Steeves."

Ordaz lifted one eyebrow. "Yes, of course. We shall have to investigate Mr. Steeves."

"How did he get that call from, uh, 36A? Bedside phone or pocket phone? Maybe he was already on the roof."

"I don't remember that he said. But we have pictures of his taxi landing."

"He had a taxi clicker. He could have just called it down."

"One more thing," I said, and Porter looked at me hopefully. "Porter, what about the elevator? It had a brain in it, didn't it? It wouldn't take anyone up unless they were on its list."

"Or unless Uncle Ray buzzed down. There's an intercom in the lobby. But at that time of night he probably wouldn't let anyone up unless he was expecting him."

"So if Sinclair was expecting a business associate, he or she was probably in the tape. How about going down? Would the elevator take you down to the lobby if you weren't in the tape?"

"I'd . . . think so."

"It would," said Ordaz. "The elevator screens entrances, not departures."

"Then why didn't the killer use it? I don't mean Steeves, necessarily. I mean *anyone,* whoever it might have been. Why didn't he just go down in the elevator? Whatever he did do, that had to be easier."

They looked at each other, but they didn't say anything.

"Okay." I turned to Ordaz. "When you check out the people in the tape, see if any of them shows a damaged arm. The killer might have pulled the same stunt Janice did: ruined her arm trying to turn off the generator. And I'd like a look at who's in that tape."

"Very well," said Ordaz, and we moved toward the squad car under the carport. We were out of earshot when he added, "How does the ARM come into this,

Mr. Hamilton? Why your interest in the murder aspect of this case?"

I told him what I'd told Bera: that Sinclair's killer might be the only living expert on Sinclair's time machine. Ordaz nodded. What he'd really wanted to know was: could I justify giving orders to the Los Angeles Police Department in a local matter? And I had answered: yes.

The rather simple-minded security system in Sinclair's elevator had been built to remember the thumbprints and the facial bone structures (which it scanned by deep-radar, thus avoiding the problems raised by changing beard styles and masquerade parties) of up to one hundred people. Most people know about a hundred people, plus or minus ten or so. But Sinclair had only listed a dozen, including himself.

RAYMOND SINCLAIR
ANDREW PORTER
JANICE SINCLAIR
EDWARD SINCLAIR SR.
EDWARD SINCLAIR III
HANS DRUCKER
GEORGE STEEVES
PAULINE URTHIEL
BERNATH PETERFI
LAWRENCE MUHAMMAD ECKS
BERTHA HALL
MURIEL SANDUSKY

Valpredo had been busy. He'd been using the police car and its phone setup as an office while he guarded the roof. "We know who some of these are," he said. "Edward Sinclair Third, for instance, is Edward Senior's grandson, Janice's brother. He's in the Belt, in Ceres, making something of a name for himself as an industrial designer. Edward Senior is Raymond's brother. He lives in Kansas City. Hans Drucker and Bertha Hall and Muriel Sandusky all live in the Greater Los Angeles area; we don't know what their connection with Sinclair is. Pauline Urthiel and Bernath Peterfi are technicians of sorts. Ecks is Sinclair's patent attorney."

"I suppose we can interview Edward Third by phone." Ordaz made a face. A phone call to the Belt wasn't cheap. "These others—"

I said, "May I make a suggestion?"

"Of course."

"Send me along with whoever interviews Ecks and Peterfi and Urthiel. They probably knew Sinclair in a business sense, and having an ARM along will give you a little more clout to ask a little more detailed questions."

"I could take those assignments," Valpredo volunteered.

"Very well." Ordaz still looked unhappy. "If this list were exhaustive I would be grateful. Unfortunately we must consider the risk that Doctor Sinclair's visitor simply used the intercom in the lobby and asked to be let in."

Bernath Peterfi wasn't answering his phone.

We got Pauline Urthiel via her pocket phone. A brusque contralto voice, no picture. We'd like to talk to her in connection with a murder investigation; would she be at home this afternoon? No. She was lecturing that afternoon, but would be home around six.

Ecks answered dripping wet and not smiling. So sorry to get you out of a shower, Mr. Ecks. We'd like to talk to you in connection with a murder investigation—

"Sure, come on over. Who's dead?"

Valpredo told him.

"Sinclair? *Ray* Sinclair? You're sure?"

We were.

"Oh, lord. Listen, he was working on something important. An interstellar drive, if it works out. If there's any possibility of salvaging the hardware—"

I reassured him and hung up. If Sinclair's patent attorney thought it was a star drive . . . maybe it was.

"Doesn't sound like he's trying to steal it," said Valpredo.

"No. And even if he'd got the thing, he couldn't have claimed it was his. If he's the killer, that's not what he was after."

We were moving at high speed, police-car speed. The car was on automatic, of course, but it could need manual override at any instant. Valpredo concentrated on the passing scenery and spoke without looking at me.

"You know, you and the Detective-Inspector aren't looking for the same thing."

"I know. I'm looking for a hypothetical killer. Julio's looking for a hypothetical visit. It could be tough to prove there wasn't one, but if Porter and the girl were telling the truth, maybe Julio can prove the visitor didn't do it."

"Which would leave the girl," he said.

"Whose side are you on?"

"Nobody's. All I've got is interesting questions." He looked at me sideways. "But you're pretty sure the girl didn't do it."

"Yah."

"Why?"

"I don't know. Maybe because I don't think she's got the brains. It wasn't a simple killing."

"She's Sinclair's niece. She can't be a complete idiot."

"Heredity doesn't work that way. Maybe I'm kidding myself. Maybe it's her arm. She's lost an arm; she's got enough to worry about." And I borrowed the car phone to dig into records in the ARM computer.

PAULINE URTHIEL. Born Paul Urthiel. Ph.D. in plasma physics, University of California at Ervine. Sex change and legal name change, 2111. Six years ago she'd been in competition for a Nobel prize, for research into the charge suppression effect in the Slaver disintegrator. Height: 5′ 9″. Weight: 135. Married Lawrence Muhammad Ecks, 2117. Had kept her (loosely speaking) maiden name. Separate residences.

BERNATH PETERFI. Ph.D. in subatomics and related fields, MIT. Diabetic. Height: 5′ 8″. Weight: 145. Application for exemption to the Fertility Laws denied, 2119. Married 2118, divorced 2122. Lived alone.

LAWRENCE MUHAMMAD ECKS. Masters degree in physics. Member of the bar. Height: 6′ 1″. Weight: 190. Artificial left arm. Vice-President, CET (Committee to End Transplants).

Valpredo said: "Funny how the human arm keeps cropping up in this case."

"Yah." Including one human ARM who didn't really belong there. "Ecks has a masters. Maybe he could have talked people into thinking the generator was his. Or maybe he thought he could."

"He didn't try to snow *us*."

"Suppose he blew it last night? He wouldn't necessarily want the generator lost to humanity, now would he?"

"How did he get out?"

I didn't answer.

Ecks lived in a tapering tower almost a mile high. At one time Lindstetter's Needle must have been the biggest thing ever built, before they started with the arcologies. We landed on a pad a third of the way up, then took a drop shaft ten floors down.

He was dressed when he answered the door, in blazing yellow pants and a net shirt. His skin was very dark, and his hair was a puffy black dandelion with threads of grey in it. On the phone screen I hadn't been able to tell which arm was which, and I couldn't now. He invited us in, sat down and waited for the questions.

Where was he last night? Could he produce an alibi? It would help us considerably.

"Sorry, nope. I spent the night going through a rather tricky case. You wouldn't appreciate the details."

I told him I would. He said, "Actually, it involves Edward Sinclair—Ray's great-nephew. He's a Belt immigrant, and he's done an industrial design that could be adapted to Earth. Swivel for a chemical rocket motor. The trouble is it's not *that* different from existing designs, it's just *better*. His Belt patent is good, but the UN laws are different. You wouldn't believe the legal tangles."

"Is he likely to lose out?"

"No, it just might get sticky if a firm called FireStorm decides to fight the case. I want to be ready for that. In a pinch I might even have to call the kid back to Earth. I'd hate to do that, though. He's got a heart condition."

Had he made any phone calls, say to a computer, during his night of research?

Ecks brightened instantly. "Oh, sure. Constantly, all night. Okay, I've got an alibi."

No point in telling him that such calls could have been made from anywhere. Valpredo asked, "Do you have any idea where your wife was last night?"

"No, we don't live together. She lives three hundred stories over my head. We've got an open marriage . . . maybe too open," he added wistfully.

There seemed a good chance that Raymond Sinclair was expecting a visitor last night. Did Ecks have any idea—?

"He knew a couple of women," said Ecks. "You might ask them. Bertha Hall is about eighty, about Ray's age. She's not too bright, not by Ray's standards, but she's as much of a physical fitness nut as he is. They go backpacking, play tennis, maybe sleep together, maybe not. I can give you her address. Then there's Muriel something. He had a crush on her a few years ago. She'd be thirty now. I don't know if they still see each other or not."

Did Sinclair know other women?

Ecks shrugged.

Who did he know professionally?

"Oh, lord, that's an endless list. Do you know anything about the way Ray worked?" He didn't wait for an answer. "He used computer setups mostly. Any experiment in his field was likely to cost millions, or more. What he was good at was setting up a computer analogue of an experiment that would tell him what he wanted to know. Take, oh . . . I'm sure you've heard of the Sinclair molecule chain."

Hell, yes. We'd used it for towing in the Belt; nothing else was light enough and strong enough. A loop of it was nearly invisibly fine, but it would cut steel.

"He didn't start working with chemicals until he was practically finished. He told me he spent four years doing molecular designs by computer analogue. The tough part was the ends of the molecule chain. Until he got that the chain would start disintegrating from the endpoints the minute you finished making it. When he finally had what he wanted, he hired an industrial chemical lab to make it for him.

"That's what I'm getting at," Ecks continued. "He hired other people to do the concrete stuff, once he knew what he had. And the people he hired had to know what they were doing. He knew the top physicists and chemists and field theorists everywhere on Earth and in the Belt."

Like Pauline? Like Bernath Peterfi?

"Yah, Pauline did some work for him once. I don't think she'd do it again. She didn't like having to give him all the credit. She'd rather work for herself. I don't blame her."

Could he think of anyone who might want to murder Raymond Sinclair?

Ecks shrugged. "I'd say that was your job. Ray never liked splitting the credit with anyone. Maybe someone he worked with nursed a grudge. Or maybe someone was trying to steal this latest project of his. Mind you, I don't know much about what he was trying to do, but if it worked it would have been fantastically valuable, and not just in money."

Valpredo was making noises like he was about finished. I said, "Do you mind if I ask a personal question?"

"Go ahead."

"Your arm. How'd you lose it?"

"Born without it. Nothing in my genes, just a bad prenatal situation. I came out with an arm and a turkey wishbone. By the time I was old enough for a transplant, I knew I didn't want one. You want the standard speech?"

"No, thanks, but I'm wondering how good your artificial arm is. I'm carrying a transplant myself."

Ecks looked me over carefully for signs of moral degeneration. "I suppose you're also one of those people who keep voting the death penalty for more and more trivial offenses?"

"No, I—"

"After all, if the organ banks ran out of criminals you'd be in trouble. You might have to live with your mistakes."

"No, I'm one of those people who blocked the second corpsicle law, kept that group from going into the organ banks. And I hunt organleggers for a living. But I don't have an artificial arm, and I suppose the reason is that I'm squeamish."

"Squeamish about being part mechanical? I've heard of that," Ecks said. "But you can be squeamish the other way, too. What there is of me is all me, not part of a dead man. I'll admit the sense of touch isn't quite the same, but it's just as good. And—look."

He put a hand on my upper forearm and squeezed.

It felt like the bones were about to give. I didn't scream, but it took an effort. "That isn't all my strength," he said. "And I could keep it up all day. This arm doesn't get tired."

He let go.

I asked if he would mind my examining his arms. He didn't. But then, Ecks didn't know about my imaginary hand.

I probed the advanced plastics of Ecks' false arm, the bone and muscle structure of the other. It was the real arm I was interested in.

When we were back in the car Valpredo said, "Well?"

"Nothing wrong with his real arm," I said. "No scars."

Valpredo nodded.

But the bubble of accelerated time wouldn't hurt plastic and batteries, I thought. And if he'd been planning to lower fifty pounds of generator two stories down on a nylon line, his artificial arm had the strength for it.

We called Peterfi from the car. He was in. He was a small man, dark-complected, mild of face, his hair straight and shiny black around a receding hairline. His eyes blinked and squinted as if the light were too bright, and he had the scruffy look of a man who has slept in his clothes. I wondered if we had interrupted an afternoon nap.

Yes, he would be glad to help the police in a murder investigation.

Peterfi's condominium was a slab of glass and concrete set on a Santa Monica cliff face. His apartment faced the sea. "Expensive, but worth it for the view," he said, showing us to chairs in the living room. The drapes were closed against the afternoon sun. Peterfi had changed clothes. I noticed the bulge in his upper left sleeve, where an insulin capsule and automatic feeder had been anchored to the bone of the arm.

"Well, what can I do for you? I don't believe you mentioned who had been murdered."

Valpredo told him.

He was shocked. "Oh, my. Ray Sinclair. But there's no telling how this will affect—" and he stopped suddenly.

"Please go on," said Valpredo.

"We were working on something together. Something —revolutionary."

An interstellar drive?

He was startled. He debated with himself, then, "Yes. It was supposed to be secret."

We admitted having seen the machine in action. How did a time compression field serve as an interstellar drive?

"That's not exactly what it is," Peterfi said. Again he debated with himself. Then, "There have always been a few optimists around who thought that just because mass and inertia have always been associated in human experience, it need not be a universal law. What Ray and I have done is to create a condition of low inertia. You see—"

"An inertialess drive!"

Peterfi nodded vigorously at me. "Essentially yes. Is the machine intact? If not—"

I reassured him on that point.

"That's good. I was about to say that if it had been destroyed, I could recreate it. I did most of the work of building it. Ray preferred to work with his mind, not with his hands."

Had Peterfi visited Sinclair last night?

"No. I had dinner at a restaurant down the coast, then came home and watched the holo wall. What times do I need alibis for?" he asked jokingly.

Valpredo told him. The jokingly look turned into a nervous grimace. No, he'd left the Mail Shirt just after nine; he couldn't prove his whereabouts after that time.

Had he any idea who might have wanted to murder Raymond Sinclair?

Peterfi was reluctant to make outright accusations. Surely we understood. It might be someone he had worked with in the past, or someone he'd insulted. Ray thought most of humanity were fools. Or—we might look into the matter of Ray's brother's exemption.

Valpredo said, "Edward Sinclair's exemption? What about it?"

"I'd really prefer that you get the story from someone else. You may know that Edward Sinclair was refused the right to have children because of an inherited heart condition. His grandson has it too. There is some question as to whether he really did the work that earned him the exemption."

"But that must have been forty to fifty years ago. How could it figure in a murder now?"

Peterfi explained patiently. "Edward had a child by virtue of an exemption to the Fertility Laws. Now there are two grandchildren. Suppose the matter came up for review? His grandchildren would lose the right to have children. They'd be illegitimate. They might even lose the right to inherit."

Valpredo was nodding. "Yah. We'll look into that, all right."

I said, "You applied for an exemption yourself not long ago. I suppose your, uh——"

"Yes, my diabetes. It doesn't interfere with my life at all. Do you know how long we've been using insulin to handle diabetes? Almost two hundred years! What does it matter if I'm a diabetic? If my children are?"

He glared at us, demanding an answer. He got none.

"But the Fertility Laws refuse me children. Do you know that I lost my wife because the Board refused me an exemption? I deserved it. My work on plasma flow in the solar photosphere— Well, I'd hardly lecture you on the subject, would I? But my work can be used to predict the patterns of proton storms near any G-type star. Every colony world owes something to my work!"

That was an exaggeration, I thought. Proton storms affected mainly asteroidal mining operations . . . "Why don't you move to the Belt?" I asked. "They'd honor you for your work, and they don't have Fertility Laws."

"I get sick off Earth. It's biorhythms; it has nothing to do with diabetes. Half of humanity suffers from biorhythm upset."

I felt sorry for the guy. "You could still get the exemption. For your work on the inertialess drive. Wouldn't that get you your wife back?"

"I . . . don't know. I doubt it. It's been two years. In any case, there's no telling which way the Board will jump. I thought I'd have the exemption last time."

"Do you mind if I examine your arms?"

He looked at me. "What?"

"I'd like to examine your arms."

"That seems a most curious request. Why?"

"There seems a good chance that Sinclair's killer damaged his arm last night. Now, I'll remind you that I'm acting in the name of the UN Police. If you've been hurt by the side effects of a possible space drive, one that might be used by human colonists, then you're concealing evidence in a—" I stopped, because Peterfi had stood up and was taking off his tunic.

He wasn't happy, but he stood still for it. His arms looked all right. I ran my hands along each arm, bent the joints, massaged the knuckles. Inside the flesh I ran my imaginary fingertips along the bones.

Three inches below the shoulder joint the bone was knotted. I probed the muscles and tendons . . .

"Your right arm is a transplant," I said. "It must have happened about six months ago."

He bridled. "You may not be aware of it, but surgery to re-attach my own arm would show the same scars."

"Is that what happened?"

Anger made his speech more precise. "Yes. I was performing an experiment, and there was an explosion. The arm was nearly severed. I tied a tourniquet and got to a 'doc before I collapsed."

"Any proof of this?"

"I doubt it. I never told anyone of this accident, and the 'doc wouldn't keep records. In any case, I think the burden of proof would be on you."

"Uh huh."

Peterfi was putting his tunic back on. "Are you quite finished here? I'm deeply sorry for Ray Sinclair's death, but I don't see what it could possibly have to do with my stupidity of six months ago."

I didn't either. We left.

Back in the car. It was seventeen twenty; we could pick up a snack on the way to Pauline Urthiel's place. I told Valpredo, "I think it was a transplant. And he didn't want to admit it. He must have gone to an organlegger."

"Why would he do that? It's not that tough to get an arm from the public organ banks."

I chewed that. "You're right. But if it was a normal transplant, there'll be a record. Well, it could have happened the way he said it did."

"Uh huh."

"How about this? He was doing an experiment, and it was illegal. Something that might cause pollution in a city, or even something to do with radiation. He picked up radiation burns in his arm. If he'd gone to the public organ banks he'd have been arrested."

"That would fit too. Can we prove it on him?"

"I don't know. I'd like to. He might tell us how to find whoever he dealt with. Let's do some digging: maybe we can find out what he was working on six months ago."

Pauline Urthiel opened the door the instant we rang. "Hi! I just got in myself. Can I make you drinks?"

We refused. She ushered us into a smallish apartment with a lot of fold-into-the-ceiling furniture. A sofa and coffee table were showing now; the rest existed as outlines on the ceiling. The view through the picture window was breathtaking. She lived near the top of Lindstetter's Needle, some three hundred stories up from her husband.

She was tall and slender, with a facial structure that would have been effeminate on a man. On a woman it was a touch masculine. The well-formed breasts might be flesh or plastic, but surgically implanted in either case.

She finished making a large drink and joined us on the couch. And the questions started.

Had she any idea who might have wanted Raymond Sinclair dead?

"Not really. How did he die?"

"Someone smashed in his skull with a poker," Valpredo said. If he wasn't going to mention the generator, neither was I.

"How quaint." Her contralto turned acid. "His own poker, too, I presume. Out of his own fireplace rack. What you're looking for is a traditionalist." She peered at us over the rim of her glass. Her eyes were large, the lids decorated in semi-permanent tattoo as a pair of flapping UN flags. "That doesn't help much, does it? You might try whoever was working with him on whatever his latest project was."

That sounded like Peterfi, I thought. But Valpredo said, "Would he necessarily have a collaborator?"

"He generally works alone at the beginning. But somewhere along the line he brings in people to figure out how to make the hardware, and make it. He never made anything real by himself. It was all just something in a computer bank. It took someone else to make it real. And he never gave credit to anyone."

Then his hypothetical collaborator might have found out how little credit he was getting for his work, and— But Urthiel was shaking her head. "I'm talking about a psychotic, not someone who's really been cheated. Sinclair never *offered* anyone a share in anything he did. He always made it damn plain what was happening. I knew what I was doing when I set up the FyreStop prototype for him, and I knew what I was doing when I quit. It was all him. He was using my training, not my brain. I wanted to do something original, something *me*."

Did she have any idea what Sinclair's present project was?

"My husband would know. Larry Ecks, lives in this same building. He's been dropping cryptic hints, and when I want more details he has this grin—" She grinned herself, suddenly. "You'll gather I'm interested. But he won't say."

Time for me to take over, or we'd never get certain questions asked. "I'm an ARM. What I'm about to tell you is secret," I said. And I told her what we knew of Sinclair's generator. Maybe Valpredo was looking at me disapprovingly; maybe not.

"We know that the field can damage a human arm in a few seconds. What we want to know," I said, "is whether the killer is now wandering around with a half-decayed hand or arm—or foot, for that—"

She stood and pulled the upper half of her body stocking down around her waist.

She looked very much a real woman. If I hadn't known—and why would it matter? These days the sex change operation is elaborate and perfect. Hell with it; I was on duty. Valpredo was looking nonchalant, waiting for me.

I examined both her arms with my eyes and my three hands. There was nothing. Not even a bruise.

"My legs too?"

I said, "Not if you can stand on them."

Next question. Could an artificial arm operate within the field?

"Larry? You mean *Larry?* You're out of your teeny mind."

"Take it as a hypothetical question."

She shrugged. "Your guess is as good as mine. There aren't any experts on inertialess fields."

"There was one. He's dead," I reminded her.

"All I know is what I learned watching the Gray Lensman show in the holo wall when I was a kid." She smiled suddenly. "That old space opera—"

Valpredo laughed. "You too? I used to watch that show in study hall on a little pocket phone. One day the Principal caught me at it."

"Sure. And then we outgrew it. Too bad. Those inertialess ships . . . I'm sure an inertialess ship wouldn't behave like those did. You couldn't possibly get rid of the time compression effect." She took a long pull on her drink, set it down and said, "Yes and no. He could reach in, but—you see the problem? The nerve impulses that move the motors in Larry's arm, they're coming into the field too slowly."

"Sure."

"But if Larry closed his fist on something, say, and reached into the field with it, it would probably stay closed. He could have brained Ray with—No, he couldn't. The poker wouldn't be moving any faster than a glacier. Ray would just dodge."

And he couldn't pull a poker out of the field, either. His fist wouldn't close on it after it was inside. But he could have tried, and still left with his arm intact, I thought.

Did Urthiel know anything of the circumstances surrounding Edward Sinclair's exemption?

"Oh, that's an old story," she said. "Sure, I heard about it. How could it possibly have anything to do with, with Ray's murder?"

"I don't know," I confessed. "I'm just thrashing around."

"Well, you'll probably get it more accurately from the UN files. Edward Sinclair did some mathematics on the fields that scoop up interstellar hydrogen for the cargo ramrobots. He was a shoo-in for the exemption. That's the surest way of getting it: make a breakthrough in anything that has anything to do with the interstellar colonies. Every time you move one man away from Earth, the population drops by one."

"What was wrong with it?"

"Nothing anyone could prove. Remember, the Fertility Restriction Laws were new then. They couldn't stand a real test. But Edward Sinclair's a pure math man. He works with number theory, not practical applications. I've seen Edward's equations, and they're closer to something Ray would come up with. And Ray didn't need the exemption. He never wanted children."

"So you think—"

"I don't *care* which of them redesigned the ramscoops. Diddling the Fertility Board like that, that takes *brains.*" She swallowed the rest of her drink, set the glass down. "Breeding for brains is never a mistake. It's no challenge to the Fertility Board either. The people who do the damage are the ones who go into hiding when their shots come due, have their babies, then scream to high heaven when the Board has to sterilize them. Too many of those and we won't have Fertility Laws any more. And *that*—" She didn't have to finish.

Had Sinclair known that Pauline Urthiel was once Paul?

She stared. "Now just what the bleep has that got to do with anything?"

I'd been toying with the idea that Sinclair might have been blackmailing Urthiel with that information. Not for money, but for credit in some discovery they'd made together. "Just thrashing around," I said.

"Well . . . all right. I don't know if Ray knew or not. He never raised the subject, but he never made a pass either, and he must have researched me before he hired me. And, say, listen: Larry doesn't know. I'd appreciate it if you wouldn't blurt it out."

"Okay."

"See, he had his children by his first wife. I'm not denying him children . . . Maybe he married me because I had a touch of, um, masculine insight. Maybe. But he doesn't know it, and he doesn't want to. I don't know whether he'd laugh it off or kill me."

I had Valpredo drop me off at ARM Headquarters. *This peculiar machine really does bother me, Gil* . . . Well it should, Julio. The Los Angeles Police were not trained to deal with a mad scientist's nightmare running quietly in the middle of a murder scene.

Granted that Janice wasn't the type. Not for this murder. But Drew Porter was precisely the type to evolve a perfect murder around Sinclair's generator, purely as an intellectual exercise. He might have guided her through it; he might even have been there, and used the elevator before she shut it off. It was the one thing he forgot to tell her: not to shut off the elevator.

Or: he outlined a perfect murder to her, purely as a puzzle, never dreaming she'd go through with it—badly.

Or: one of them had killed Janice's uncle on impulse. No telling what he'd said that one of them couldn't tolerate. But the machine had been right there in the living room, and Drew had wrapped his big arm around Janice and said, *Wait, don't do anything yet, let's think this out* . . .

Take any of these as the true state of affairs, and a prosecutor could have a hell of a time proving it. He could show that no killer could possibly have left the scene of the crime without Janice Sinclair's help, and therefore . . . But what about that glowing thing, that time machine built by the dead man? *Could* it have freed a killer from an effectively locked room? How could a judge know its power?

Well, could it?

Bera might know.

The machine was running. I caught the faint violet glow as I stepped into the laboratory, and a flickering next to it . . . and then it was off, and Jackson Bera stood suddenly beside it, grinning, silent, waiting.

I wasn't about to spoil his fun. I said, "Well? Is it an interstellar drive?"

"Yes!"

A warm glow spread through me. I said, "Okay."

"It's a low intertia field," said Bera. "Things inside lose most of their inertia . . . not their mass, just the resistance to movement. Ratio of about five hundred to one. The interface is sharp as a razor. We think there are quantum levels involved."

"Uh huh. The field doesn't affect time directly?"

"No, it . . . I shouldn't say that. Who the hell knows what time really is? It affects chemical and nuclear reactions, energy release of all kinds . . . but it doesn't affect the speed of light. You know, it's kind of kicky to be measuring the speed of light at three hundred and seventy miles per second with honest instruments."

Dammit. I'd been half-hoping it was an FTL drive. I said, "Did you ever find out what was causing that blue glow?"

Bera laughed at me. "Watch." He'd rigged a remote switch to turn the machine on. He used it, then struck a match and flipped it toward the blue glow. As it crossed an invisible barrier the match flared violet-white for something less than an eyeblink. I blinked. It had been like a flashbulb going off.

I said, "Oh, *sure*. The machinery's warm."

"Right. The blue glow is just infrared radiation being boosted to violet when it enters normal time."

Bera shouldn't have had to tell me that. Embarrassed, I changed the subject. "But you said it was an interstellar drive."

"Yah. It's got drawbacks," said Bera. "We can't just put a field around a whole starship. The crew would think they'd lowered the speed of light, but so what? A slowboat doesn't get that close to lightspeed anyway. They'd save a little trip time, but they'd have to live through it five hundred times as fast."

"How about if you just put the field around your fuel tanks?"

Bera nodded. "That's what they'll probably do. Leave the motor and the life support system outside. You could carry a godawful amount of fuel that way . . . Well, it's not our department. Someone else'll be designing the starships," he said a bit wistfully.

"Have you thought of this thing in relation to robbing banks? Or espionage?"

"If a gang could afford to build one of these jobs, they wouldn't need to rob banks." He ruminated. "I hate making anything this big a UN secret. But I guess you're right. The average government could afford a whole stable of the things."

"Thus combining James Bond and the Flash."

He rapped on the plastic frame. "Want to try it?"

"Sure," I said.

Heart to brain: THUD! What're you doing? You'll get us all killed! I knew we should never have put you in charge of things . . . I stepped up to the generator, waited for Bera to scamper beyond range, then pulled the switch.

Everything turned deep red. Bera became as a statue.

Well, here I was. The second hand on the wall clock had stopped moving. I took two steps forward and rapped with my knuckles. Rapped, hell: it was like rapping on contact cement. The invisible wall was tacky.

I tried leaning on it for a minute or so. That worked fine until I tried to pull away, and then I knew I'd done something stupid. I was embedded in the interface. It took me another minute to pull loose, and then I went sprawling backward; I'd picked up too much inward velocity, and it all came into the field with me.

At that I'd been lucky. If I'd leaned there a little longer I'd have lost my leverage. I'd have been sinking deeper and deeper into the interface, unable to yell to Bera, building up more and more velocity outside the field.

I picked myself up and tried something safer. I took out my pen and dropped it. It fell normally: thirty-two feet per second per second, field time. Which scratched one theory as to how the killer had thought he would be leaving.

I switched the machine off. "Something I'd like to try," I told Bera. "Can you hang the machine in the air, say by a cable around the frame?"

"What have you got in mind?"

"I want to try standing on the bottom of the field."

Bera looked dubious.

It took us twenty minutes to set it up. Bera took no

chances. He lifted the generator about five feet. Since the field seemed to center on that oddly shaped piece of silver, that put the bottom of the field just a foot in the air. We moved a stepladder into range, and I stood on the stepladder and turned on the generator.

I stepped off.

Walking down the side of the field was like walking in progressively stickier taffy. When I stood on the bottom I could just reach the switch.

My shoes were stuck solid. I could pull my feet out of them, but there was no place to stand except in my own shoes. A minute later my feet were stuck too: I could pull one loose, but only by fixing the other ever more deeply in the interface. I sank deeper, and all sensation left the soles of my feet. It was scary, though I knew nothing terrible could happen to me. My feet wouldn't die out there; they wouldn't have time.

But the interface was up to my ankles now, and I started to wonder what kind of velocity they were building up out there. I pushed the switch up. The lights flashed bright, and my feet slapped the floor hard.

Bera said, "Well? Learn anything?"

"Yah. I don't want to try a real test: I might wreck the machine."

"What kind of real test—?"

"Dropping it forty stories with the field on. Quit worrying, I'm not going to do it."

"Right. You aren't."

"You know, this time compression effect would work for more than just spacecraft. After you're on the colony world you could raise full grown cattle from frozen fertilized eggs in just a few minutes."

"Mmm . . . Yah." The happy smile flashing white against darkness, the infinity look in Bera's eyes . . . Bera liked playing with ideas. "Think of one of these mounted on a truck, say on Jinx. You could explore the shoreline regions without ever worrying about the bandersnatchi attacking. They'd never move fast enough. You could drive across any alien world and catch the whole ecology laid out around you, none of it running from the truck. Predators in mid-leap, birds in mid-flight, couples in courtship."

"Or larger groups."

"I . . . think that habit is unique to humans." He looked at me sideways. "You wouldn't spy on *people*, would you? Or shouldn't I ask?"

"That five-hundred-to-one ratio. Is that constant?"

He came back to here and now. "We don't know. Our theory hasn't caught up to the hardware it's supposed to fit. I wish to hell we had Sinclair's notes."

"You were supposed to send a programmer out there—"

"He came back," Bera said viciously. "Clayton Wolfe. Clay says the tapes in Sinclair's computer were all wiped before he got there. I don't know whether to believe him or not. Sinclair was a secretive bastard, wasn't he?"

"Yah. One false move on Clay's part and the computer might have wiped everything. But he says different, hmmm?"

"He says the computer was blank, a newborn mind all ready to be taught. Gil, is that possible? Could whoever have killed Sinclair have wiped the tapes?"

"Sure, why not? What he couldn't have done is left afterward." I told him a little about the problem. "It's even worse than that, because as Ordaz keeps pointing out, he thought he'd be leaving with the machine. I thought he might have been planning to roll the generator off the roof, step off with it and float down. But that wouldn't work. Not if it falls five hundred times as fast. He'd have been killed."

"Losing the machine maybe saved his life."

"But *how did he get out?*"

Bera laughed at my frustration. "Couldn't his niece be the one?"

"Sure, she could have killed her uncle for the money. But I can't see how she'd have a motive to wipe the computer. Unless—"

"Something?"

"Maybe. Never mind." Did Bera ever miss this kind of manhunting? But I wasn't ready to discuss this yet; I didn't know enough. "Tell me more about the machine. Can you vary that five-hundred-to-one ratio?"

He shrugged. "We tried adding more batteries. We thought it might boost the field strength. We were wrong; it just expanded the boundary a little. And using one less battery turns it off completely. So the ratio seems to be constant, and there do seem to be quantum levels involved. We'll know better when we build another machine."

"How so?"

"Well, there are all kinds of good questions," said Bera. "What happens when the fields of two generators intersect? They might just add, but maybe not. That quantum effect . . . And what happens if the generators are right next to each other, operating in each other's accelerated time? The speed of light could drop to a few feet per second. Throw a punch and your hand gets shorter!"

"That'd be kicky, all right."

"Dangerous, too. Man, we'd better try that one on the Moon!"

"I don't see that."

"Look, with one machine going, infrared light comes out violet. If two machines were boosting each other's performance, what kind of radiation would they put out? Anything from X-rays to antimatter particles."

"An expensive way to build a bomb."

"Well, but it's a bomb you can use over and over again."

I laughed. "We did find you an expert," I said. "You may not need Sinclair's tapes. Bernath Peterfi says he was working with Sinclair. He could be lying—more likely he was working *for* him, under contract—but at least he knows what the machine does."

Bera seemed relieved at that. He took down Peterfi's address. I left him there in the laboratory, playing with his new toy.

The file from City morgue was sitting on my desk, open, waiting for me since this morning. Two dead ones looked up at me through sockets of blackened bone; but not accusingly. They had patience. They could wait.

The computer had processed my search pattern. I braced myself with a cup of coffee, then started leafing through the thick stack of printout. When I knew what had burned away two human faces, I'd be close to knowing who. Find the tool, find the killer. And the tool must be unique, or close to it.

Lasers, lasers—more than half the machine's suggestions seemed to be lasers. Incredible, the way lasers seemed to breed and mutate throughout human industry. Laser radar. The laser guidance system on a tunneling machine. Some suggestions were obviously unworkable . . . and one was a lot too workable.

A standard hunting laser fires in pulses. But it can be jiggered for a much longer pulse or even a continuous burst.

Set a hunting laser for a long pulse, and put a grid over the lens. The mesh has to be optically fine, on the order of angstroms. Now the beam will spread as it leaves the grid. A second of pulse will vaporize the grid, leaving no evidence. The grid would be no bigger than a contact lens; if you didn't trust your aim you could carry a pocketful of them.

The grid-equipped laser would be less efficient, as a rifle with a silencer is less efficient. But the grid would make the murder weapon impossible to identify.

I thought about it and got cold chills. Assassination is already a recognized branch of politics. If this got out —But that was the trouble; someone seemed to have thought of it already. If not, someone would. Someone always did.

I wrote up a memo for Lucas Garner. I couldn't think of anyone better qualified to deal with this kind of sociological problem.

Nothing else in the stack of printout caught my eye. Later I'd have to go through it in detail. For now, I pushed it aside and punched for messages.

Bates, the coroner, had sent me another report. They'd finished the autopsies on the two charred corpses. Nothing new. But Records had identified the fingerprints. Two missing persons, disappeared six and eight months ago. Ah HA!

I knew that pattern. I didn't even look at the names; I just skipped on to the gene coding.

Right. The fingerprints did not match the genes. All twenty fingertips must be transplants. And the man's scalp was a transplant; his own hair had been blond.

I leaned back in my chair, gazing fondly down at holographs of charred skulls.

You evil sons of bitches. Organleggers, both of you.

With all that raw material available, most organleggers change their fingerprints constantly—and their retina prints; but we'd never get prints from those charred eyeballs. So: weird weapon or no, they were ARM business. My business.

And we still didn't know what had killed them, or who.

It could hardly have been a rival gang. For one thing, there was no competition. There must be plenty of business for every organlegger left alive after the ARM had swept through them last year. For another, why had they been dumped on a city slidewalk? Rival organleggers would have taken them apart for their own organ banks. Waste not, want not.

On that same philosophy, I had something to be deeply involved in when the mother hunt broke. Sinclair's death wasn't ARM business, and his time compression field wasn't in my field. This was both.

I wondered what end of the business the dead ones had been in. The file gave their estimated ages: forty for the man, forty-three for the woman, give or take three years each. Too old to be raiding the city street for donors. That takes youth and muscle. I billed them as doctors, culturing the transplants and doing the operations; or salespersons, charged with quietly letting prospective clients know where they could get an operation without waiting two years for the public organ banks to come up with material.

So: they'd tried to sell someone a new kidney and been killed for their impudence. That would make the killer a hero.

So why hide them for three days, then drag them out onto a city slidewalk in the dead of night?

Because they'd been killed with a fearsome new weapon?

I looked at the burnt faces and thought: fearsome, right. Whatever did that *had* to be strictly a murder weapon. As the optical grid over a laser lens would be strictly a murder technique.

So: a secretive scientist and his deformed assistant, fearful of rousing the wrath of the villagers, had dithered over the bodies for three days, then disposed of them in that clumsy fashion because they panicked when the bodies started to smell. Maybe.

But a prospective client needn't have used his shiny new terror weapon. He had only to call the cops after they were gone. It read better if the killer was a prospective *donor;* he'd fight with anything he could get his hands on.

I flipped back to full shots of the bodies. They looked to be in good condition. Not much flab. You don't collect a donor by putting an armlock on him; you use a needle gun. But you still need muscle to pick up the body and move it to your car, and you have to do that damn quick. Hmmm . . .

Someone knocked at my door.

I shouted, "Come on in!"

Drew Porter came in. He was big enough to fill the office, and he moved with a grace he must have learned on a board. "Mr. Hamilton? I'd like to talk to you."

"Sure. What about?"

He didn't seem to know what to do with his hands. He looked grimly determined. "You're an ARM," he said. "You're not actually investigating Uncle Ray's murder. That's right, isn't it?"

"That's right. Our concern is with the generator. Coffee?"

"Yes, thanks. But you know all about the killing. I thought I'd like to talk to you, straighten out some of my own ideas."

"Go ahead." I punched for two coffees.

"Ordaz thinks Janice did it, doesn't he?"

"Probably. I'm not good at reading Ordaz' mind. But it seems to narrow down to two distinct groups of possible killers. Janice and everyone else. Here's your coffee."

"Janice didn't do it." He took the cup from me, gulped at it, set it down on my desk and forgot about it.

"Janice and X," I said. "But X couldn't have left. In fact, X couldn't have left even if he'd had the machine he came for. And we still don't know why he didn't just take the elevator."

He scowled as he thought that through. "Say he had a way to leave," he said. "He wanted to take the machine —he *had* to want that, because he tried to use the machine to set up an alibi. But even if he couldn't take the machine, he'd still use his alternate way out."

"Why?"

"It'd leave Janice holding the bag, if he knew Janice was coming home. If he didn't, he'd be leaving the police with a locked room mystery."

"Locked room mysteries are good clean fun, but I never heard of one happening in real life. In fiction they usually happen by accident." I waved aside his protest. "Never mind. You argue well. But what was his alternate escape route?"

Porter didn't answer.

"Would you care to look at the case against Janice Sinclair?"

"She's the only one who could have done it," he said bitterly. "But she didn't. She couldn't kill anyone, not that cold-blooded, pre-packaged way, with an alibi all set up and a weird machine at the heart of it. Look, that machine is too *complicated* for Janice."

"No, she isn't the type. But—no offense intended— you are."

He grinned at that. "Me? Well, maybe I am. But why would I want to?"

"You're in love with her. I think you'd do anything for her. Aside from that, you might enjoy setting up a perfect murder. And there's the money."

"You've got a funny idea of a perfect murder."

"Say I was being tactful."

He laughed at that. "All right. Say I set up a murder for the love of Janice. Damn it, if she had that much hate in her I wouldn't love her! Why would she want to kill Uncle Ray?"

I dithered as to whether to drop that on him. Decided *yes*. "Do you know anything about Edward Sinclair's exemption?"

"Yah, Janice told me something about . . ." He trailed off.

"Just what did she tell you?"

"I don't have to say."

That was probably intelligent. "All right," I said. "For the sake of argument, let's assume it was Raymond Sinclair who worked out the math for the new ramrobot scoops, and Edward took the credit, with Raymond's connivance. It was probably Raymond's idea. How would that sit with Edward?"

"I'd think he'd be grateful forever," said Porter. "Janice says he is."

"Maybe. But people are funny, aren't they? Being grateful for fifty years could get on a man's nerves. It's not a natural emotion."

"You're so young to be so cynical," Porter said pityingly.

"I'm trying to think this out like a prosecution lawyer. If these brothers saw each other too often Edward might get to feeling embarrassed around Raymond. He'd have a hard time relaxing with him. The rumors wouldn't help . . . oh, yes, there are rumors. I've been told that Edward couldn't have worked out those equations because he doesn't have the ability. If that kind of thing got back to Edward, how would he like it? He might even start avoiding his brother. Then Ray might remind brother Edward of just how much he owed him . . . and that's the kiss of death."

"Janice says no."

"Janice could have picked up the hate from her father. Or she might have started worrying about what would happen if Uncle Ray changed his mind one day. It could happen any time, if things were getting strained between the elder Sinclairs. So one day she shut his mouth—"

Porter growled in his throat.

"I'm just trying to show you what you're up against. One more thing: the killer may have wiped the tapes in Sinclair's computer."

"Oh?" Porter thought that over. "Yah. Janice could have done that just in case there were some notes in there, notes on Ed Sinclair's ramscoop field equations. But, look: X could have wiped those tapes too. Stealing the generator doesn't do him any good unless he wipes it out of Uncle Ray's computer."

"True enough. Shall we get back to the case against X?"

"With pleasure." He dropped into a chair. Watching his face smooth out, I added, *and with great relief*.

I said, "Let's not call him X. Call him K for killer." We already had an Ecks involved . . . and his family name probably *had* been X, once upon a time. "We've been assuming K set up Sinclair's time compression effect as an alibi."

Porter smiled. "It's a lovely idea. *Elegant,* as a mathematician would say. Remember, I never saw the actual murder scene. Just chalk marks."

"It was—macabre. Like a piece of surrealism. A very bloody practical joke. K could have deliberately set it up that way, if his mind is twisted enough."

"If he's that twisted, he probably escaped by running himself down the garbage disposal."

"Pauline Urthiel thought he might be a psychotic. Someone who worked with Sinclair, who thought he wasn't getting enough credit." Like Peterfi, I thought, or Pauline herself.

"I like the alibi theory."

"It bothers me. Too many people knew about the machine. How did he expect to get away with it? Lawrence Ecks knew about it. Peterfi knew enough about the machine to rebuild it from scratch. Or so he says. You and Janice saw it in action."

"Say he's crazy then. Say he hated Uncle Ray enough to kill him and then set him up in a makeshift Dali painting. He'd still have to get *out*." Porter was working his hands together. The muscles bulged and rippled in his arms. "This whole thing depends on the elevator, doesn't it? If the elevator hadn't been locked and on Uncle Ray's floor, there wouldn't be a problem."

"So?"

"So. Say he did leave by elevator. Then Janice came home, and she automatically called the elevator up and locked it. She does that without thinking. She had a bad shock last night. This morning she didn't remember."

"And this evening it could come back to her."

Porter looked up sharply. "I wouldn't—"

"You'd better think long and hard before you do. If Ordaz is sixty percent sure of her now, he'll be a hundred percent sure when she lays that on him."

Porter was working his muscles again. In a low voice he said, "It's possible, isn't it?"

"Sure. It makes things a lot simpler, too. But if Janice said it now, she'd sound like a liar."

"But it's *possible*."

"I give up. Sure, it's possible."

"Then who's our killer?"

There wasn't any reason I shouldn't consider the question. It wasn't my case at all. I did, and presently I laughed. "Did I say it'd make things simpler? Man, it throws the case *wide open! Anyone* could have done it. Uh, anyone but Steeves. Steeves wouldn't have had any reason to come back this morning."

Porter looked glum. "Steeves wouldn't have done it anyway."

"He was your suggestion."

"Oh, in pure mechanical terms, he's the only one who didn't need a way out. But—you don't know Steeves. He's a big, brawny guy with a beer belly and no brains. A nice guy, you understand, I *like* him, but if he ever killed anyone it'd be with a beer bottle. And he was proud of Uncle Ray. He liked having Raymond Sinclair in his building."

"Okay, forget Steeves. Is there anyone you'd particularly like to pin it on? Bearing in mind that now *anyone* could get in to do it."

"Not anyone. Anyone in the elevator computer, plus anyone Uncle Ray might have let up."

"Well?"

He shook his head.

"You make a hell of an amateur detective. You're afraid to accuse anyone."

He shrugged, smiling, embarrassed.

"What about Peterfi? Now that Sinclair's dead, he can claim they were equal partners in the, uh, time machine. And he tumbled to it awfully fast. The moment Valpredo told him Sinclair was dead, Peterfi was his partner."

"Sounds typical."

"Could he be telling the truth?"

"I'd say he's lying. Doesn't make him a killer, though."

"No. What about Ecks? If he didn't know Peterfi was involved, he might have tried the same thing. Does he need money?"

"Not hardly. And he's been with Uncle Ray for longer than I've been alive."

"Maybe he was after the Immunity. He's had kids,

but not by his present wife. He may not know she can't have children."

"Pauline *likes* children. I've seen her with them." Porter looked at me curiously. "I don't see having children as that big a motive."

"You're young. Then there's Pauline herself. Sinclair knew something about her. Or Sinclair might have told Ecks, and Ecks blew up and killed him for it."

Porter shook his head. "In red rage? I can't think of anything that'd make Larry do that. Pauline, maybe. Larry, no."

But, I thought, there are men who would kill if they learned that their wives had gone through a sex change. I said, "Whoever killed Sinclair, if he wasn't crazy, he had to want to take the machine. One way might have been to lower it by rope . . ." I trailed off. Fifty pounds or so, lowered two stories by nylon line. Ecks' steel and plastic arm . . . or the muscles now rolling like boulders in Porter's arms. I thought Porter could have managed it.

Or maybe he'd thought he could. He hadn't actually had to go through with it.

My phone rang.

It was Ordaz. "Have you made any progress on the time machine? I'm told that Dr. Sinclair's computer—"

"Was wiped, yah. But that's all right. We're learning quite a lot about it. If we run into trouble, Bernath Peterfi can help us. He helped build it. Where are you now?"

"At Dr. Sinclair's apartment. We had some further questions for Janice Sinclair."

Porter twitched. I said, "All right, we'll be right over. Andrew Porter's with me." I hung up and turned to Porter. "Does Janice know she's a suspect?"

"No. Please don't tell her unless you have to. I'm not sure she could take it."

I had the taxi drop us at the lobby level of the Rodewald Building. When I told Porter I wanted a ride in the elevator, he just nodded.

The elevator to Raymond Sinclair's penthouse was a box with a seat in it. It would have been comfortable for one, cozy for two good friends. With me and Porter in it it was crowded. Porter hunched his knees and tried to fold into himself. He seemed used to it.

He probably was. Most apartment elevators are like that. Why waste room on an elevator shaft when the same space can go into apartments?

It was a fast ride. The seat was necessary; it was two gee going up and a longer period at half a gee slowing down, while lighted numbers flickered past. Numbers, but no doors.

"Hey, Porter. If this elevator jammed, would there be a door to let us out?"

He gave me a funny look and said he didn't know. "Why worry about it? If it jammed at this speed it'd come apart like a handful of shredded lettuce."

It was just claustrophobic enough to make me wonder. K hadn't left by elevator. Why not? Because the ride up had terrified him? *Brain to memory: dig into the medical records of that list of suspects. See if any of them have records of claustrophobia.* Too bad the elevator brain didn't keep records. We could find out which of them had used the boxlike elevator once or not at all.

In which case we'd be looking for K_2. By now I was thinking in terms of three groups. K_1 had killed Sinclair, then tried to use the low-inertia field as both loot and alibi. K_2 was crazy; he hadn't wanted the generator at all, except as a way to set up his macabre tableau. K_3 was Janice and Drew Porter.

Janice was there when the doors slid open. She was wan and her shoulders slumped. But when she saw Porter she smiled like sunlight and ran to him. Her run was wobbly, thrown off by the missing weight of her arm.

The wide brown circle was still there in the grass, marked with white chalk and the yellow chemical that picks up bloodstains. White outlines to mark the vanished body, the generator, the poker.

Something knocked at the back door of my mind. I looked from the chalk outlines, to the open elevator, to the chalk . . . and a third of the puzzle fell into place.

So simple. We were looking for K_1 . . . and I had a pretty good idea who he was.

Ordaz was asking me, "How did you happen to arrive with Mr. Porter?"

"He came to my office. We were talking about a hypothetical killer—" I lowered my voice slightly. "—a killer who isn't Janice."

"Very good. Did you reason out how he must have left?"

"Not yet. But play the game with me. Say there was a way."

Porter and Janice joined us, their arms about each other's waists. Ordaz said, "Very well. We assume there was a way out. Did he improvise it? And why did he not use the elevator?"

"He must have had it in mind when he got here. He didn't use the elevator because he was planning to take the machine. It wouldn't have fit."

They all stared at the chalk outline of the generator. So simple. Porter said, "Yah! Then he used it anyway, and left you a locked room mystery!"

"That may have been his mistake," Ordaz said grimly. "When we know his escape route we may find that only one man could have used it. But of course we do not even know that the route exists."

I changed the subject. "Have you got everyone on the elevator tape identified?"

Valpredo dug out his spiral notebook and flipped to the jotted names of those people permitted to use Sinclair's elevator. He showed it to Porter. "Have you seen this?"

Porter studied it. "No, but I can guess what it is. Let's see . . . Hans Drucker was Janice's lover before I came along. We still see him. In fact, he was at that beach party last night at the Randalls'."

"He flopped on the Randalls' rug last night," said Valpredo. "Him and four others. One of the better alibis."

"Oh, *Hans* wouldn't have anything to do with this!" Janice exclaimed. The idea horrified her.

Porter was still looking at the list. "You know about most of these people already. Bertha Hall and Muriel Sandusky were lady friends of Uncle Ray's. Bertha goes backpacking with him."

"We interviewed them too," Valpredo told me. "You can hear the tapes if you like."

"No, just give me the gist. I already know who the killer is."

Ordaz raised his eyebrows at that, and Janice said, "Oh, good! Who?" which question I answered with a secretive smile. Nobody actually called me a liar.

Valpredo said, "Muriel Sandusky's been living in England for almost a year. Married. Hasn't seen Sinclair in years. Big, beautiful redhead."

"She had a crush on Uncle Ray once," said Janice. "And vice versa. I think his lasted longer."

"Bertha Hall is something else again," Valpredo continued. "Sinclair's age, and in good shape. Wiry. She says that when Sinclair was on the home stretch on a project he gave up everything: friends, social life, exercise. Afterward he'd call Bertha and go backpacking with her to catch up with himself. He called her two nights ago and set a date for next Monday."

I said, "Alibi?"

"Nope."

"Really!" Janice said indignantly. "Why, we've known Bertha since I was that high! If you know who killed Uncle Ray, why don't you just say so?"

"Out of this list, I sure do, given certain assumptions. But I don't know how he got out, or how he expected to, or whether we can prove it on him. I can't accuse anyone *now*. It's a damn shame he didn't lose his arm reaching for that poker."

Porter looked frustrated. So did Janice.

"You would not want to face a lawsuit," Ordaz suggested delicately. "What of Sinclair's machine?"

"It's an inertialess drive, sort of. Lower the inertia, time speeds up. Bera's already learned a lot about it, but it'll be awhile before he can really . . ."

"You were saying?" Ordaz asked when I trailed off.

"Sinclair was *finished* with the damn thing."

"Sure he was," said Porter. "He wouldn't have been showing it around otherwise."

"Or calling Bertha for a backpacking expedition. Or spreading rumors about what he had. Yeah. Sure, he knew everything he could learn about that machine. Julio, you were cheated. It all depends on the machine. And the bastard did wrack up his arm, and we can prove it on him."

We were piled into Ordaz' commandeered taxi: me and Ordaz and Valpredo and Porter. Valpredo had set the thing for conventional speeds so he wouldn't have to worry about driving. We'd turned the interior chairs to face each other.

"This is the part I won't guarantee," I said, sketching rapidly in Valpredo's borrowed notebook. "But remember, he had a length of line with him. He must have expected to use it. Here's how he planned to get out."

I sketched in a box to represent Sinclair's generator, a stick-figure clinging to the frame. A circle around them to represent the field. A bow knot tied to the machine, with one end trailing up through the field.

"See it? He goes up the stairs with the field on. The camera has about one chance in eight of catching him while he's moving at that speed. He wheels the machine to the edge of the roof, ties the line to it, throws the line a good distance away, pushes the generator off the roof and steps off with it. The line falls at thirty-two feet per second squared, normal time, plus a little more because the machine and the killer are tugging down on it. Not hard, because they're in a low-inertia field. By the time the killer reaches ground he's moving at something more than, uh, twelve hundred feet per second over five hundred . . . uh, say three feet per second internal time, and he's got to pull the machine out of the way fast, because the rope is going to hit like a bomb."

"It looks like it would work," said Porter.

"Yah. I thought for a while that he could just stand on the bottom of the field. A little fooling with the machine cured me of that. He'd smash both legs. But he could hang onto the frame; it's strong enough."

"But he didn't have the machine," Valpredo pointed out.

"That's where you got cheated. What happens when two fields intersect?"

They looked blank.

"It's not a trivial question. Nobody knows the answer yet. *But Sinclair did.* He had to, he was *finished.* He must have had two machines. The killer took the second machine."

Ordaz said, "Ahh."

Porter said, "Who's K?"

We were settling on the carport. Valpredo knew where we were, but he didn't say anything. We left the taxi and headed for the elevators.

"That's a lot easier," I said. "He expected to use the machine as an alibi. That's silly, considering how many people knew it existed. But if he didn't know that Sinclair was ready to start showing it to people—specifically to you and Janice—who's left? Ecks only knew it was some kind of interstellar drive."

The elevator was uncommonly large. We piled into it.

"And," said Valpredo, "there's the matter of the arm. I think I've got that figured too."

"I gave you enough clues," I told him.

Peterfi was a long time answering our buzz. He may have studied us through the door camera, wondering why a parade was marching through his hallway. Then he spoke through the grid. "Yes? What is it?"

"Police. Open up," said Valpredo.

"Do you have a warrant?"

I stepped forward and showed my ident to the camera. "I'm an ARM. I don't need a warrant. Open up. We won't keep you long." *One way or another*.

He opened the door. He looked neater now than he had this afternoon, despite informal brown indoor pajamas. "Just you," he said. He let me in, then started to close the door on the others.

Valpredo put his hand against the door. "Hey—"

"It's okay," I said. Peterfi was smaller than I was, and I had a needle gun. Valpredo shrugged and let him close the door.

My mistake. I had two-thirds of the puzzle, and I thought I had it all.

Peterfi folded his arms and said, "Well? What is it you want to search this time? Would you like to examine my legs?"

"No, let's start with the insulin feeder on your upper arm."

"Certainly," he said, and startled hell out of me.

I waited while he took off his shirt—unnecessary, but he needn't know that—then ran my imaginary fingers through the insulin feed. The reserve was nearly full. "I

should have known," I said. "Dammit. You got six
months worth of insulin from the organlegger."

His eyebrows went up. "Organlegger?" He pulled
loose. "Is this an accusation, Mr. Hamilton? I'm taping
this for my attorney."

And I was setting myself up for a lawsuit. The hell
with it. "Yah, it's an accusation. You killed Sinclair.
Nobody else could have tried that alibi stunt."

He looked puzzled—honestly, I thought. "Why not?"

"If anyone else had tried to set up an alibi with Sinclair's generator, Bernath Peterfi would have told the
police all about what it was and how it worked. But you
were the only one who knew that, until last night, when
he started showing it around."

There was only one thing he could say to that kind of
logic, and he said it. "Still recording, Mr. Hamilton."

"Record and be damned. There are other things we
can check. Your grocery delivery service. Your water
bill."

He didn't flinch. He was smiling. Was it a bluff? I
sniffed the air. Six months worth of body odor emitted
in one night? By a man who hadn't taken more than
four or five baths in six months? But his air conditioning
was too good.

The curtains were open now to the night and the
ocean. They'd been closed this afternoon, and he'd been
squinting. But it wasn't evidence. The lights: he only
had one light burning now, and so what?

The big, powerful campout flashlight sitting on a
small table against a wall. I hadn't even noticed it this
afternoon. Now I was sure I knew what he'd used it
for . . . but how to prove it?

Groceries . . . "If you didn't buy six months' worth
of groceries last night, you must have stolen them. Sinclair's generator is perfect for thefts. We'll check the local supermarkets."

"And link the thefts to me? How?"

He was too bright to have kept the generator. But
come to think of it, where could he abandon it? He was
guilty. He couldn't have covered *all* his tracks—

"Peterfi? I've got it."

He believed me. I saw it in the way he braced himself. Maybe he'd worked it out before I did. I said,

"Your contraceptive shots must have worn off six months early. Your organlegger couldn't get you that; he's got no reason to keep contraceptives around. You're dead, Peterfi."

"I might as well be. Damn you, Hamilton! You've cost me the exemption!"

"They won't try you right away. We can't afford to lose what's in your head. You know too much about Sinclair's generator."

"Our generator! We built it together!"

"Yah."

"You won't try me at all," he said more calmly. "Are you going to tell a court how the killer left Ray's apartment?"

I dug out my sketch and handed it to him. While he was studying it I said, "How did you like going off the roof? You couldn't have *known* it would work."

He looked up. His words came slowly, reluctantly. I guess he had to tell someone, and it didn't matter now. "By then I didn't care. My arm hung like a dead rabbit, and it stank. It took me three minutes to reach the ground. I thought I'd die on the way."

"Where'd you dig up an organlegger that fast?"

His eyes called me a fool. "Can't you guess? Three years ago. I was hoping diabetes could be cured by a transplant. When the government hospitals couldn't help me I went to an organlegger. I was lucky he was still in business last night."

He drooped. It seemed all the anger went out of him. "Then it was six months in the field, waiting for the scars to heal. In the dark. I tried taking that big campout flashlight in with me." He laughed bitterly. "I gave that up after I noticed the walls were smoldering."

The wall above that little table had a scorched look. I should have wondered about that earlier.

"No baths," he was saying. "I was afraid to use up that much water. No exercise, practically. But I had to eat, didn't I? And all for nothing."

"Will you tell us how to find the organlegger you dealt with?"

"This is your big day, isn't it, Hamilton? All right, why not. It won't do you any good."

"Why not?"

He looked up at me very strangely.

Then he spun about and ran.

He caught me flatfooted. I jumped after him. I didn't know what he had in mind; there was only one exit to the apartment, excluding the balcony, and he wasn't headed there. He seemed to be trying to reach a blank wall . . . with a small table set against it, and a camp flashlight on it and a drawer in it. I saw the drawer and thought, *gun!* And I surged after him and got him by the wrist just as he reached the wall switch above the table.

I threw my weight backward and yanked him away from there . . . and then the field came on.

I held a hand and arm up to the elbow. Beyond was a fluttering of violet light: Peterfi thrashing frantically in a low-inertia field. I hung on while I tried to figure out what was happening.

The second generator was here somewhere. In the wall? The switch seemed to have been recently plastered in, now that I saw it close. Figure a closet on the other side, and the generator in it. Peterfi must have drilled through the wall and fixed that switch. Sure, what else did he have to do with six months of spare time?

No point in yelling for help. Peterfi's soundproofing was too modern. And if I didn't let go Peterfi would die of thirst in a few minutes.

Peterfi's feet came straight at my jaw. I threw myself down, and the edge of a boot sole nearly tore my ear off. I rolled forward in time to grab his ankle. There was more violet fluttering, and his other leg thrashed wildly outside the field. Too many conflicting nerve impulses were pouring into the muscles. The leg flopped about like something dying. If I didn't let go he'd break it in a dozen places.

He'd knocked the table over. I didn't see it fall, but suddenly it was lying on its side. The top, drawer included, must have been well beyond the field. The flashlight lay just beyond the violet fluttering of his hand.

Okay. He couldn't reach the drawer; his hand wouldn't get coherent signals if it left the field. I could let go of his ankle. He'd turn off the field when he got thirsty enough.

And if I didn't let go, he'd die in there.

It was like wrestling a dolphin one-handed. I hung on anyway, looking for a flaw in my reasoning. Peterfi's free leg seemed broken in at least two places . . . I was about to let go when something must have jarred together in my head.

Faces of charred bone grinned derisively at me.

Brain to hand: HANG ON! Don't you understand? He's trying to reach the flashlight!

I hung on.

Presently Peterfi stopped thrashing. He lay on his side, his face and hands glowing blue. I was trying to decide whether he was playing possum when the blue light behind his face quietly went out.

I let them in. They looked it over. Valpredo went off to search for a pole to reach the light switch. Ordaz asked, "Was it necessary to kill him?"

I pointed to the flashlight. He didn't get it.

"I was overconfident," I said. "I shouldn't have come in alone. He's already killed two people with that flashlight. The organleggers who gave him his new arm. He didn't want them talking, so he burned their faces off and then dragged them out onto a slidewalk. He probably tied them to the generator and then used the line to pull it. With the field on the whole setup wouldn't weigh more than a couple of pounds."

"With a flashlight?" Ordaz pondered. "Of course. It would have been putting out five hundred times as much light. A good thing you thought of that in time."

"Well, I do spend more time dealing with these odd-ball science fiction devices than you do."

"And welcome to them," said Ordaz.

AFTERWORD

The Last Word About SF Detectives

They said it couldn't be done. Even John W. Campbell, editor of *Analog,* said it couldn't be done. Campbell was often right. This time he irritated a writer named Hal Clement into writing the first detective science-fiction novel . . . to Campbell's intense satisfaction.

After *Needle* there were others. Alfred Bester wrote *The Demolished Man,* a police procedural set in a society of telepaths. Isaac Asimov has for some time been writing of two series detectives, Dr. Wendell Urth and Lije Bailey, very different men living in very different eras. Lately Randall Garrett has been writing of an armchair detective, Lord Darcy, from a world where magic is a developed science with its own mathematics and special tools. I have read detective science fiction in *Ellery Queen's Mystery Magazine*: fair puzzles set in believable futures.

And of course there were failures . . .

I tried it myself. I was working on ARM, the third story in this volume, before ever I sold a story. I had sold a few to Fred Pohl of *Galaxy* before I finished ARM, and I sent that primitive version to him, and was turned down. Then I sent it to John W. Campbell, Jr., and was turned down.

What came of that was two letters lecturing me on why detective science fiction is so difficult to write, and what was wrong with ARM in particular.

I can admit it now: that early version of ARM was bad. There were too many characters; there were holes in both the science and the sociology; the puzzle grew far too complex. I was young and naive. I had not seen that 'tec/stf stories are rare, and for a reason.

The trouble is that there are two sets of rules to be followed.

A detective story is a puzzle. In theory at least, the reader can know what crime was committed, by whom, and how and where and why, before he is given the answer. There must be only one possible answer. Enough data must have been given to make it obviously true.

Science fiction is an exercise in imagination. It should be believable, granted; but a believable story can be dull. In general, the more interesting an idea, the less it needs to be justified. A story is judged on its internal consistency and the reach of the author's imagination. Strange backgrounds, odd societies following odd laws, unfamiliar values and ways of thinking are the rule.

Now, how can the reader anticipate the author if all the rules are strange? If science fiction recognizes no limits, then . . . perhaps the victim was death-wished from outside a locked room, or the walls may be permeable to an X-ray laser. Perhaps the alien's motivation really is beyond comprehension. Can the reader really rule out time travel? Invisible killers? Some new device tinkered together by a homicidal genius?

More to the point, how can I *give* you a fair puzzle? With great difficulty, that's how. There's nothing impossible about it. In a locked room mystery you can trust John Dickson Carr not to ring in a secret passageway. You can trust me too. If there's an X-ray laser involved, I'll tell you so. If I haven't mentioned an invisible man, there isn't one. If the ethics of Belt society are important, I will have gone into detail on the subject.

Detective and science fiction (and fantasy and crime fiction) do have a lot in common. Readers, for one: both genres attract readers who like a challenge, a puzzle. Whether it's the odd disappearance of a weapon (a glass dagger hidden in a flower vase of water) or the incomprehensibly violent behavior of a visiting alien (he needs a rest room, *bad*), the basic question is *What's going on?* The reader is entitled to his chance to outthink the author.

Much detective fiction is also sociological fiction . . . as is much science fiction . . . as are Asimov's 'tec/stf novels *The Caves of Steel* and *The Naked Sun,* and Brunner's *Puzzle on Tantalus.* Bester's *The Demolished Man* is that, and is also an involuted psychological study, a subject well suited to its society of telepaths. Well, psychological studies are common in detective fiction. So are puzzles in basic science . . . and Asimov's Wendell Urth stories fit in that group. Garrett's Lord Darcy operates in a world of working magic, but the stories are puzzles in internal consistency. Ellery Queen would feel at home with them.

In the mixed marriage of mystery and science fiction there are pitfalls. A '50s novel of matter duplicators, *Double Jeopardy,* suffered from internal inconsistency: a coin reversed except for the lettering, an error in multiplication . . . Edward Hoch writes good tight puzzle stories for mystery fiction fans, but in his near-future mystery "The Transvection Machine" he warped his sociology beyond credibility to make a tighter puzzle. It's a subtler trap.

I did the same with ARM.

So I put ARM away until I should learn more about my craft . . .

My first published 'tec/stf story was to have been a parody. I got to wondering: what would a private eye of Sam Spade's clan do if, as he was approaching the climax of a case . . . as, having worked out who and how, he was preparing to pit his life against the guns and guile of the villain . . . he learned that he was being studied by an obtrusive alien anthropologist?

Only, it didn't work out as parody. There was already too much of the science fiction writer in me. Internal consistency is all. Tough Bruce Cheseborough, Jr., defended his two-valued universe well and vigorously. He solved a fair puzzle in time to save his life, though it was way outside his field. I like Cheseborough. I have always gotten too involved with my characters.

I damn well did in "Death by Ecstasy."

You see, I don't usually write of pure black-hearted villains. Loren the organlegger was my first. I finished the first draft of that story at six o'clock one morning . . . went to bed . . . stared at the ceiling . . . gave up about ten and went out looking for friends. I found some. I found Joyce MacDaniel to massage my back. She said the muscles were rigid as iron.

Same story for the second draft, except that I gave up earlier: stared at the ceiling from six to eight, got up and made breakfast. The killing of Loren was a very rough experience. It may not shake you, but it shook me.

That was the first of the tales of Gil the ARM of the Amalgamated Regional Militia, the police force of the United Nations. The acronym came first. I had to make up words and background to fit the initials. And the ending came first; I built backward from a simple how-does-he-get-out-of-it.

The second story bubbled in my head for a long time before I wrote down anything but notes.

The Bouchercon is a gathering of detective fiction fans now held annually in memory of Anthony Boucher, long-time editor of *Ellery Queen's Mystery Magazine* and *Fantasy and Science Fiction,* and the author of a gem of a crime/stf story, "Nine Finger Jack." At the time of the first Bouchercon I had worked out the crime in "The Defenseless Dead," a most unusual crime with a most unusual motive, and I outlined that crime to an audience during a panel discussion. I knew the crime before I knew how to write about it. "The Defenseless Dead" was meticulously plotted in advance, and it didn't hit me nearly as hard as "Death by Ecstasy." Maybe it should have. The story and the assumptions behind it are terrifying, and uncomfortably reasonable.

I generally write more than one story set in a given future. It isn't laziness. Honest, it isn't laziness. It's just that, having designed a detailed, believable, even probable future, I often find that I have more to say about it than will fit in one story.

So it comes about that Gil the ARM lives and works in the twenty-one twenties of the *known space* line of history, whose story runs from 1,500,000,000 years in the past to 1200 years in the future and occupies half a million words as of this writing. Most of these novels and short stories occur within a region of space thirty light years across (*human space*), but lines of development extend two hundred light years up along galactic north, and thirty-three thousand light years to the galactic core.

Somewhere in there I wrote five stories set in a different future, in which cheap teleportation was developed in the 1980s. There were sociological fiction, but two, "The Alibi Machine" and "A *Kind* of Murder," were mysteries. The assumption of a world-wide network of instant transportation booths does imply new kinds of crime and, particularly, a new kind of killer. He's the guy who would otherwise have moved away to another city. Now he finds himself living next door, effectively, to his boss and his business rival and his ex-wife and the guy who has owed him thirty bucks for six years and denies it. Where can he go? So he kills.

These stories count as practice. Ten years afterward, with half a dozen 'tec/stf stories under my scalp, I was ready to have another look at ARM.

ARM looked bad. I had to rewrite from scratch. I saved what I could: some nice paragraphs of description, including the surrealist murder scene, and a couple of the characters, and the strongest bones in the plot skeleton. I took out a lot of verbal thrashing about in outré restaurants. Gil the ARM replaced his boss, Lucas Garner, as the detective involved. I took out a coin-operated automatic surgeon capable of implanting the bud of a new organ: it didn't fit the era, and it made things too easy for the killer. I took out an irrelevant nightmare. (Too much Ellery Queen influence on the young Larry Niven.) There was a gadget called the FyreStop device, which killed by suppressing chemical reactions: a fun thing, but unnecessary, and it complicated the bejeesus out of the plot. Losing that cost me three or four suspects, and good riddance.

Then I showed the rewritten story to Jerry Pournelle. He made me rewrite it. Among less important flaws he showed me where the organleggers came in.

In general, then, I corrected the flaws John Campbell had pointed out in a twelve page letter. I wish he'd lived to see it. I wanted his respect. I finally did sell Campbell a story, but I wish he'd seen this one.

How likely is this future that is Gil Hamilton's present? Less likely than it used to be. I don't see how we can avoid the overcrowding or the rigid, dictatorial population control without the blessing of a major war. But the organ bank problem is something else again.

For it does seem that the most useful, the most probably successful, organ transplants would come from healthy donors. And it does seem a remarkable thing, almost divinely ordained, if you look at it right, that your average ax murderer could actually save more lives than he took, if he can be disassembled for transplants. The damn trouble is that the same statement applies equally to a drunk driver. Even if he hasn't hit anyone yet. Or to a chronic pickpocket, or an over-tactless critic of government policy.

Also your average voter would probably like to go on living, given the choice. If his best choice is a transplanted heart or kidney, and there aren't any, what will he vote to be the next capital crime? Am I being over-cynical about my fellow man?

Possibly I am. What matters is that it may not matter. Our sick voter has other choices. By 2120 A.D. his new heart may well be built of plastic and wire, with tiny batteries and tiny pumps. It may work better than the original model, and be less likely to be rejected by immune reactions, which seems to be the fate of heart transplants.

Or, the surest way to prevent a transplant from being rejected might be to take it from a clone of the patient: a tissue culture treated to grow as a human being, then grown to adulthood. All tissues compatible. No immune reaction. Of course, this matter of clones raises its own ethical problems. A clone is *human* unless, as has happened before, society redefines *human*.

The organ bank problem used to scare me. The internal logic seems so rigid. But if it were *that* obvious, the Red Cross would have been finding its blood donors on Death Row, five quarts to a donor, since 1940 A.D. That has not been happening. Perhaps I'm making a big deal out of nothing.

Maybe it only took someone to point out the advantages. In which case blame it all on Larry Niven.